## THEIR LIPS MET IN
## A BURST OF DIZZYING SENSATIONS....

Marcy felt a delicious heat shudder through
her body as Drew's arms brought her close,
and as she leaned into him, she realized that
she'd never felt quite like this before. Slowly,
his mouth began to explore hers with a lazy,
sensuous movement, and her lips parted.

With a shallow gasp, Marcy turned her head
to one side but still clung to him, her body
swaying unsteadily with the roll of the boat.
And as he slid his hands upward from her
waist, she felt herself dissolving. . . .

KATHRYN KENT has been self-employed since she
graduated from Kent State University with a degree in
accounting. A few years ago, she sold her vending-machine
business, took a creative-writing course at her alma mater,
and has been writing full-time ever since. Ms. Kent lives in
Uniontown, Ohio, and has three grown children: all very
close, all tremendously supportive. She is the author of
two other Rapture Romances, *Precious Possession* and *Silk
and Steel*.

Dear Reader:

We at Rapture Romance hope you will continue to enjoy our four books each month as much as we enjoy bringing them to you. Our commitment remains strong to giving you only the best, by well-known favorite authors and exciting new writers.

We've used the comments and opinions we've heard from *you*, the reader, to make our selections, so please keep writing to us. Your letters have already helped us bring you better books—the kind you want—and we appreciate and depend on them. Of course, we are always happy to forward mail to our authors—writers need to hear from their fans!

And don't miss any of the inside story on Rapture. To tell you about upcoming books, introduce you to the authors, and give you a behind-the-scenes look at romance publishing, we've started a *free* newsletter, *The Rapture Reader*. Just write to the address below, and we will be happy to send you each issue.

Happy reading!

The Editors
Rapture Romance
New American Library
1633 Broadway
New York, NY 10019

# RELUCTANT SURRENDER

*by*
### Kathryn Kent

RAPTURE ROMANCE
NEW AMERICAN LIBRARY

NAL BOOKS ARE AVAILABLE AT QUANTITY DISCOUNTS
WHEN USED TO PROMOTE PRODUCTS OR SERVICES.
FOR INFORMATION PLEASE WRITE TO PREMIUM MARKETING DIVISION,
NEW AMERICAN LIBRARY, 1633 BROADWAY,
NEW YORK, NEW YORK 10019.

Copyright © 1984 by Jean Salter Kent

SIGNET, SIGNET CLASSIC, MENTOR, PLUME, MERIDIAN AND NAL BOOKS
are published by New American Library,
1633 Broadway, New York, New York 10019

First Printing, April, 1984

1  2  3  4  5  6  7  8  9

PRINTED IN THE UNITED STATES OF AMERICA

*To Mary*

# Chapter One

Marcy hung up the phone and angrily threw her pencil on the desk, furious with the inefficiency of big business. As manager of the Fort Lauderdale branch of the sprawling Super S grocery chain, she'd just spent a good half hour on the phone trying to get someone from the main office in Tampa to send a maintenance man out to repair the frozen-food unit. After talking with three people, all she'd gotten were half promises that someone would be on the way soon. But even soon was too late.

Shoving her chair back from the desk, she stood up and looked around her office as if expecting to find an answer somewhere. It was a small glass-partitioned room near the front of the store, just behind the head cashier's station. Marcy impatiently brushed a strand of blond hair away from her face and exhaled an exasperated sigh. She was beginning to understand the frustrating feeling of helplessness that had driven so many of their top managers into other fields of work. But Marcy refused to let it get her down. At twenty-nine, she was striving to be one of Super S Markets' most conscientious, resourceful and efficient managers. In the two months she'd been at the Fort Lauderdale store, there'd been a catastrophe of some kind almost every week, and so far, she reminded herself, she'd triumphed over all of them. The present melt-down of their main freezer unit was just another episode in a long succession of mind-chilling emergencies. If she dealt with it calmly and rationally, she'd emerge the victor once again. End of pep talk.

Striding out of her office into the store area, Marcy stopped at the head cashier's elevated platform and raised her eyes to the woman above.

"Louella, if Tampa calls, I'll be in the back. I want to make sure the stock boys are putting the fast-selling food in the front of the storage freezer and the oddball stuff in back."

"Are you going to have room for everything?" Louella asked.

Marcy shook her head. "There might be if we do a lot of rearranging and jam everything in, but it's going to be one macho mess trying to find stuff for the customers."

"Oh, they'll understand," Louella assured her. "It's happened before, and no one's gotten apoplexy over it yet."

"I hope you're right." Marcy sighed as she started for the back of the store.

Stopping in front of the empty frozen-food case, she made a mental note to get someone to clean it out and post a sign instructing customers to give their frozen-food order to one of the stock boys. Hopefully, they'd be able to find—her thoughts churned to a stop as her eye caught the tall, sun-bronzed figure of the "Super S man-of-the-hour." He'd been coming into the store for over a month, and every time he did, Marcy could almost hear the fluttering of her cashiers' hearts as they fought a secret battle to woo him into their checkout lane. One cashier even posted a LANE CLOSED sign until he came into view. Then she whisked it off and signaled him over with a cheery

"I'm open, sir." Marcy had put a stop to that, telling them they'd have to take their chances.

Now that she saw him up close, Marcy had to admit that he did look like an ad for suntan oil, with his blond hair, his contrasting brown eyebrows and rangy, beautifully proportioned body. He was wearing shorts and T-shirt and a pair of worn sneakers, the usual summer attire for men in the Fort Lauderdale area.

Marcy noticed he'd turned his cart in her direction and was closing the distance between them with long, purposeful strides. He stopped when he came abreast of her, inclined his head in a slight nod, gave her a small smile and leaned forward a little to read her badge.

"You're the manager?" he asked.

"That's right."

He kept reading. "And your name is Marcy Jamison?"

"That's right."

His eyebrows lifted a fraction. "Mrs.?"

The question caught Marcy off guard, and she found herself fumbling for words. She wasn't accustomed to having strangers quiz her about her marital status. Though she'd been divorced for over a year now, she still bristled when she thought someone was trying to delve into her past. She was a private person who kept her innermost thoughts concealed behind her easy smile and dark, soulful eyes.

She turned to face her interrogator. His expression was watchful and even slightly assessing, but there was no hint of mockery there. She could understand why the cashiers were gaga over him. He was friendly, likable . . .

Suddenly, she realized she hadn't answered his question. "That's right," she said quickly. "It's Mrs."

He nodded, as though digesting the information, but Marcy knew he was weighing the pause between his question and her answer. She found herself waiting for his next query, which would undoubtedly be the standard, "And where is Mr. Jamison?" delivered with a knowing grin. The format never varied.

But he surprised her.

"Then perhaps you can tell me, Mrs. Jamison, how I go about getting a package of frozen Chinese pea pods."

Marcy blinked. "Chinese pea pods?" she repeated.

He nodded once, his expression firm and serious, as though some grave problem had suddenly arisen. But he didn't fool Marcy for a minute. Behind his implacable expression and worried little smile, she could see the dancing glint of amusement in those Nordic-blue eyes of his.

"I'm a gourmet cook," he hastened to explain. "In fact, that's why I come here. You have rare food items I can't get anyplace else." He tried to sound convincing, but it didn't go over.

"Is that right?" Marcy lowered her glance to his grocery cart. It was half filled with beer, taco chips, cold cuts and pink coconut cookies. She lifted out a can of Mexican chili and studied the label. "You specialize in Chinese cooking, you say?"

A glint of humor flashed in his eyes. "You might say that. Actually, I'm interested in all foreign foods. This just happens to be Chinese week."

She glanced meaningfully at his cart. "And what's this? Beach week?"

His recovery time was phenomenal. "No. Breakfast."

"I see." She nodded, her face absolutely expressionless. Inwardly, however, she found herself enjoying his repartee more than she cared to admit. His vitality was like a breath of fresh air. But she knew better than to succumb to his bold good looks. Experience had taught her that handsome men had a habit of using their sensual appeal to get what they wanted and most women gave it to them willingly. But Marcy wasn't most women.

She gestured toward the empty freezer. "As you can see, everything's been moved to the storage units in back. I'll have to get a stock boy to find your pea pods for you, but it might take awhile. Do you have other shopping to do?"

"No, I don't," he answered quickly. Then, as an afterthought, added, "And I'm in a hurry."

Marcy paused and, lowering her lids, took a deep breath of air. Why is it, she wondered, that the good-looking ones were always such pests?

"In that case"—she sighed dramatically—"I'll find them myself."

"In that case"—he grinned—"I'll help you look."

"Oh, no, please," she said, raising her hands in a halting gesture, "I work better alone."

He shook his head. "I don't believe that."

His gaze slid lazily down the full length of her body and up again. Marcy was tall, with a beautifully proportioned figure; unfortunately, it was always concealed beneath the regulation blue lab coat with the big gold "Super S" on the pocket. It was a dull shapeless thing, but Marcy chose it over the regulation blue blazer because it was more practical. But nothing could obscure her shapely legs or her shoulder-length wheat-blond hair that she wore loosely curled, with long wispy bangs that accentuated the luminous depths of her soft brown eyes.

Her observer lifted a questioning brow. "Do you always have to wear that jacket? It makes you look pregnant."

"Well, I'm not!" she flared indignantly. "And I'd appreciate it if you'd keep your comments to yourself." Whirling on her heel, she started for the back of the store. "I'll just be a minute," she threw over her shoulder. "Why don't you read a magazine while you're waiting? We have a nice selection of comic books."

"I've already read them." He grinned as he followed right behind her, a little closer than necessary. She could feel his eyes scanning the contours of her hips and legs.

Marcy felt uncomfortable under his close scrutiny but managed to hold back an angry retort. As she had suspected, the man was an egomaniac who thought his captivating smile was, automatically, his ticket to anywhere. She'd met people like this many times before. There was no escaping them. Self-centered, thoughtless, inconsiderate, their only distinction in life was that they were such a nuisance. Yet, she reminded herself, he was a customer and, hence, always right. To suggest that he take his shopping list elsewhere would be against company policy, and Marcy was a stickler for the rules. As manager of a store with eighty-five people working under her, she had to be.

When she reached the swinging doors leading to the stockroom, she turned to the tall figure looming behind her.

"Look, Mr.—"

"Bradford," he introduced himself.

"Look, Mr. Bradford—"

"Drew Bradford."

Suddenly a firm hand gripped her own and Marcy felt momentarily paralyzed as a new and unexpected warmth surged up her arm. For the briefest moment, she stood still, conscious of the exotic scent of his after-shave and the heat of his body as he stepped closer. Reaching a long arm around her, he swung the door open. Then, with a firm hand at her back, he guided her into the stockroom as if she was the visitor and he the manager.

As usual, the behind-the-scene section of the store was hopping with activity. The manager of general merchandise, a small, nervous man named Kenneth, was supervising the pricing of housewares and drugs. Label guns clicked incessantly as two stock boys hurried through the task of stamping each item in case after case of aspirin, tea strainers, light bulbs, shampoos and dustpans. Marcy nodded to Kenneth and was about to speak when someone started the compactor. The loud thudding noise of boxes being fed into the gaping jaws of the crusher made speech impossible. Marcy and Kenneth settled for a brief passing nod as she led her guest past him toward the walk-in freezers. A teenage boy was just removing his heavy jacket and gloves. Even in the heat of the room, the cold air still swirled around him.

"Is anyone in there?" Marcy asked, indicating the freezer.

"Yeah. Glen is." He rubbed his hands together. "Boy, what a mess! We've got french fries all over the place. Those bags popped like balloons when we moved them."

"They wouldn't have if you'd been more careful," she scolded. "Has he got everything pretty well organized?"

"As good as it'll ever be."

"Then find yourself pencil and paper and go out into the store and get the customers' orders for frozen foods." The boy nodded, grateful to be released from the frigid temperatures of the walk-in freezer. "But before you go," she added, "we have a request for a package of Chinese pea pods."

The kid's mouth gaped open. "You gotta be kiddin."

"No, unfortunately, I'm not." She couldn't help but slide a reproving glance at Drew, but he remained passively unimpressed. Here was a man who wanted his pea pods, whatever the cost.

"Better get them before you do anything else."

"Oh, Jeez," the kid grumbled, shrugging into his jacket. "They're probably buried forever."

Just as he opened the door to go back in, Glen, the manager of the frozen-food division, came out. He, too, was surrounded by a vapor of frost. He nodded to Marcy while pulling off his knitted cap, but he didn't say anything. He just shook his head in disgust.

She smiled encouragingly. "They're supposed to be here today," she said, though her voice held little hope. "In the meantime, if you need the stock boys, use them, even if they have to work overtime."

Glen nodded, slightly relieved. He started to say something, but his words were cut off by the crackle of the intercom. Louella's voice boomed into the room.

"We need a price check on alligator pears, and all the bag boys are standing out in the parking lot talking," she complained irritably. "Want me to go?"

Reaching up, Marcy flicked the "on" switch. "No, stay put. I'll take care of it." Then she turned to the first stock boy she saw. "Get that price check, will you?"

He started to protest. "But that's not my job, and I have to finish this—"

"Move!" she ordered, cutting off his complaint.

"Yes, *ma'am!*" he snapped impudently. Throwing

down his carton knife, he stomped across the room and kicked through the swinging doors into the store.

Marcy caught Drew Bradford's disapproving lift of the eyebrows. "Nice kid," he commented. "Too bad he doesn't work for your competitor."

She couldn't help but smile. Somehow, it was reassuring to be able to share even a small piece of her problems with someone else. She found herself wondering if he was in management. He seemed to be aware of her predicament and even sympathetic. Undoubtedly days like this happened in every business, but still, it was nice to know that at least one person out there understood.

Suddenly, Louella's voice penetrated the atmosphere again, this time slightly more hysterical. "Cindy's register is jammed and she's in the middle of an order. What do you want me to do?"

Marcy paused for a moment, pushing her hair back in a gesture of impatience. "How many items have gone through? More than twelve?"

"Hmmm." She could almost see Louella craning her neck to peer over the glass partition. "No, I don't think so."

"Well"—Marcy sighed—"that's the first break we've had today. Cindy's going to have to put everything back in the customer's cart and send her to another checkout lane. Tell her to take a break while we open up register seven for her."

"Gotcha."

As Marcy flicked off the switch she became aware of the all-encompassing presence of her number-one customer and suddenly realized he hadn't uttered a word of complaint in over ten minutes. In fact, he seemed so absorbed in his surroundings that he'd evidently forgotten he was in a hurry. Glancing up at him, she couldn't help but notice the tingle of excitement inside her. His deep blue eyes were studying her with a seriousness she hadn't seen before. For a long moment, she could almost feel the movement of his breathing. It sent a new and unexpected warmth through her. For all his grumbling and complaining, there was a strong thread of intelligence and under-standing in those powerful blue eyes. Had she underestimated him?

Marcy found herself wondering who he was, where he came from, what he did and, she paused, hating to admit it even to herself, whether or not he was mar-ried. Very likely. Men as good-looking as Drew Bradford didn't stay single long. But then, she shrugged inwardly, what concern was that of hers? She wasn't interested in getting involved with anyone, especially someone as handsome as he was. Undoubt-edly, he was accustomed to women who chased after him, fawned over him and treated him like a king. Marcy simply wasn't his type; the submissive, servile role had never appealed to her.

"If you want to wait here for your order, you can," she said, stepping away from him a little, "but I have to get back to the front."

"I can see why." He nodded. "Don't you have an assistant who can take on some of this responsibility?"

Marcy clasped her hands over her ears and shook her head. "Oh, please, don't even talk about it."

"That bad, huh?"

"I'll say." Marcy realized she shouldn't be complain-ing to a customer, but this one was different. He'd very likely faced the same frustrations she was encountering today. The compulsion to confide in someone who understood her dilemma was almost overwhelming, especially someone who seemed so interested, so ready to listen.

"The manager before me had two assistants," she

explained, "a part-time and a full-time. Then, a month after I got here, the company decided to cut costs, so they transferred the full-time assistant to another store. Now all I have is Larry who works the night shift."

"Surely you can demand more help, can't you?"

She pulled her mouth into a flat line and shook her head. "It's not that easy and, believe me, I know. I spent nine years in our main office in Tampa." She raised her eyes skyward. "No one would believe the politics and the red tape that's involved in a business this size."

He nodded, understanding. "*I* believe it. I'm an accountant, and I've participated in a lot of audits of businesses like this. It's the same everywhere you go," he assured her, "and if it will make you feel any better, it's going to get worse."

"I don't see how companies survive under these conditions. . . ."

"A lot of them don't. Fortunately, a few of them manage to wake up before it's too late and pull things together. Everything goes along fine for a while, then the first thing you know, they drift right back to the way they were. It's a vicious cycle that's been going on ever since the Industrial Revolution."

One corner of his mouth curved upward in a conspiratorial smile. Marcy found herself relaxing, her defenses melting, as she returned the smile with one of her own. Suddenly, she realized that she was dallying . . . and enjoying it. This was so unlike her, but Drew Bradford had a way of making her forget the crises of the moment. It was a refreshing change to discuss business with someone on a management level, something she had missed since she'd left the security of the main office where there was always someone to share her problems.

But time was wasting, she reminded herself, and the work was piling up. She started toward the swinging doors. "I'd better get back to the front before the whole place falls apart," she said with a quick smile.

He opened the door for her. She glanced up to nod her thanks, but Drew was preoccupied, his brow creased in a slight frown.

He fell into step beside her. "Don't you have any department managers?"

"Yes. Six of them."

"Can't they handle some of these problems?"

"They do the best they can, but we're open thirteen hours a day. They can't be here all the time, so if something comes up, it's the manager's job to fill in."

"Hmm." He nodded. He understood, but he didn't agree. "I think this is too much responsibility to give a woman. This is a man's job."

She stopped in midstride. "Man's job!" she spluttered, wondering where she'd ever gotten the idea he knew what he was talking about. "Who are you to decide who's capable and who isn't? Have you ever managed a supermarket before?" she challenged.

"No, but I can't see how it would vary much from any other business," he argued. "The basic procedures are the same everywhere."

"Well!" she exclaimed, trying to keep her voice low so that customers wouldn't think there was dissension in the ranks, "I'd just like to see you apply your standard modis operandi to a store like this, Mr. Bradford. You'd find out very quickly that our problems are unique and must be dealt with on a one-to-one basis."

They'd reached Marcy's office. She nodded to Louella as she went in with Drew Bradford following right behind her. Marcy could almost feel the sudden stillness in the air as all cash registers were suspended in silence for a long breathless moment. Marcy didn't have to turn around to know all eyes were on her, wondering how she'd captured the handsome Apollo. He didn't help any by standing in the doorway, hands in pockets, shoulder leaning against the doorjamb. His expression was an odd combination of amusement and confidence.

He smiled affably. "I don't want to keep you from your work any longer than necessary, but I *do* want to fill out an application for the job of assistant manager."

Marcy's eyes opened wide with astonishment. "You *what*? Oh, no." She shook her head. "You can't get a management job here unless you've worked your way up through the ranks. The Super S always promotes from within. It's a company policy."

Drew peeled himself away from the wall and sauntered into the room, pushing the door closed behind him. For a moment, Marcy felt her breath catch in her throat. He acted as if he owned the place and everyone in it, but if he thought he was going to dominate her, she fumed silently, he had another guess coming. With the long sigh of someone who'd reached the end of her patience, she swept past him to the door and pulled it open. Then she turned and faced him levelly, her eyes dark and glowering.

"I don't know about you, Mr. Bradford, but I don't like games. I suggest you pick up your pea pods and go."

His arrogance was so great that he didn't even know he'd been insulted, a fact that made Marcy even angrier. He folded his arms across his chest, leaned against Marcy's desk and crossed one foot over the other. The epitome of nonchalance and bad manners combined.

"I'm not leaving until I fill out an application," he stated firmly, once again letting his gaze rake down the full length of her body in a deliberately seductive glance. To Marcy's dismay, she felt a blush creeping into her cheeks. She tried to cover it by being as businesslike as possible.

"Legally, I can't deny you the right to apply," she stated primly. "Nor can I tell you that you don't stand the chance of a snowball in hell of landing the job. All I can do is give you an application."

She marched over to her desk, yanked open a lower drawer and pulled out an application tablet. She tore one of the sheets off, tossed the tablet back in the drawer and kicked it shut with her foot.

His eyes glistened with maddening amusement. "Temper, temper."

She thrust the paper toward him. "Here. Take this home, fill it out and mail it to the address on the back. Then I suggest you forget about it. It's doubtful you'll ever hear from the Super S."

He folded the paper carefully and put it in his shirt pocket. "I take it the home office does the hiring."

She shrugged noncommittally. "More or less."

"What does that mean?"

"They narrow the field down to three or four applicants. I choose from those."

"Hmm." He nodded thoughtfully. "That doesn't give you much leeway, does it?"

She resented the censorious tone in his voice. It was almost as if he was trying to goad her into criticizing her company. Though she was aware of many shortcomings in company management, Marcy wasn't going to confide in a customer. And that's all he was, really, a customer. Even though he filled the room with his presence and demanded every consideration due him, he was still just a customer. If she'd forgotten that fact for a moment, it was understandable, she told herself. He did have an overpowering personality and a captivating charm that would make anyone momentarily forget protocol. But for Marcy, the moment had passed. Her feet were back on the ground, her head was on her shoulders, her mind clear and in focus.

Drew started past her, but stopped at the doorway and extended his hand. She couldn't refuse to take it. As her fingers locked around his hand, Marcy felt every fiber in her body tighten with the burning heat of his grip. She swallowed hard and finally managed to speak.

"Good-bye, Mr. Bradford."

He released her hand slowly, as if reluctant to let it go. "It's Drew," he corrected, looking deep into her eyes, "and it's not good-bye."

She mumbled something appropriate, she couldn't remember what, and followed him with her eyes until he was out of sight. Then she took a deep, lung-filling breath of air. For all his arrogance and self-center-edness, Drew Bradford's charm was almost impossible to resist.

Yet resist it, she must. Despite the fact that he exuded a presence born of certainty, he was, apparently unemployed. If he was the hotshot accountant he made himself out to be, wouldn't he be in great demand? If anyone as handsome as he was had an ounce of brains, he'd have wealthy widows and divorcées swarming all over him. But then, Marcy shrugged, what did it matter to her? She'd probably never see him again—certainly not as a business part-ner. He'd never make it through the preliminary screening at Super S's main office. And even if, by some remote fluke, his name *did* filter down to her desk, she'd never hire him. Men like Drew Bradford were too arrogant to take orders from a woman, and she had enough problems without adding the complexities of a male ego to the list.

Her intercom buzzed. "That guy left without picking up his pea pods!" came the complaining voice of the frozen-food manager.

Oh hell, she thought as she flipped up the switch. "Leave them out, Glen. I'll have them for lunch."

# Chapter Two

%

It was late Friday afternoon when the compressor on the frozen-food unit was repaired. Glen and two stock boys removed everything from the storage freezers, loaded it onto uni-carts and hauled it back into the store. This inevitably caused confusion and crowding in the aisle, and customers had to skin past them sideways to get by. It wouldn't have been so bad except that many unhurried shoppers stood around to watch the restocking and offer suggestions as to where everything should go.

"Why can't we dress one of the stock boys up as a clown and let him perform tricks up at the front of the store?" Glen suggested wearily. "It would cut our restocking time in half."

"I'd like to," Marcy agreed, "but we've almost reached our maximum hour level for stock boys this week. It doesn't look like we'll have much help over the weekend."

Glen understood and just shook his head. Company policy prohibited managers from working anyone over forty hours a week. Overtime was considered an unnecessary expense and was strictly forbidden, regardless of the circumstances. The extra help needed to accommodate customers during the two-day melt-down had used up most of the allotted hours. Department managers who were already overworked would have to fill in. Marcy held her breath, wondering how long it would be before they started handing in their resignations.

With a frustrated sigh, she started back to her office. This time she went down aisle four, past soft drinks, paper plates, and other picnic supplies. Every time she went from the rear of the store to her office, she made a point of going down a different aisle, just to check it out. Not much escaped her critical eye, which was one of the reasons she was fast becoming one of Super S's most efficient store managers.

Marcy stopped for a moment to put a bag of charcoal back on the shelf. She noticed, however, that there was no room for it there, which meant that one of the stock boys had left it out in the aisle, hoping it would sell before someone tripped over it—a Super S no-no. When it came to rules and regulations, Marcy knew them all. In fact, she'd written some of them herself when she'd worked in the main office.

She took the extra bag of charcoal to the front and put it in the return bin, making a mental note to speak to Kenneth about it. Then she went into her office to make another phone call to Tampa. It would be the third of the day. As she sat down at her desk she glanced at the computer, the office register and the pile of data that had to be run before she left for the day. Without any interruptions, it would take two hours, and since she'd already been here six, it looked like another ten-hour day. The norm for management, she thought grimly, but she'd never complain.

When she and Roger were divorced over a year ago, Marcy wanted nothing more than to get as far away from Tampa as possible. Her friends, though well meaning, could never understand the split and kept trying to rationalize it, patch it up, get the model couple back together again. Only Marcy and Roger knew it would never work. When an opening suddenly came up for a store manager in Fort Lauderdale, Marcy jumped at it. It wasn't only a nice promotion for her; it would also get her out of Tampa. Her supervisor and good friend, Gail, told her to go for it if she wanted it. Though nothing was ever said, Marcy was sure that Gail had intervened on her behalf. In any case, she won out over the other applicants and landed the job. Admittedly, it looked better on paper than it did in reality, but she was determined to ride it out; Marcy was not easily discouraged.

She sat down at her desk, leaned back in her chair and dialed Gail's direct line. Her voice was as warm and enthusiastic as ever, and they talked several minutes about personal things before getting down to business.

"Have you still got one register down, honey?" Gail asked.

"We sure have," Marcy told her, "and we also have a customer injury to report."

She could almost see the older woman reaching for her pencil. "Okay, what happened?"

"Someone reached into the bottle return bin and cut their hand on a piece of broken glass."

"Did you have a caution sign posted?"

"Yes. It says: Do not reach into this bin. Employees only."

"Good. Don't worry about it. It'll never come to anything," came Gail's reassuring voice. "How's everything else?"

"Terrible," Marcy complained. "I've been working ten and eleven hours a day and I'm still behind. When am I going to get an assistant?"

"That's up to personnel." Gail sighed heavily. "Their budget is way down, you know. At least they claim it is. I'll see what I can do to hurry it up."

"You might remind them that I've already submitted thirty-one applications, and some of those
women looked good. One had had management
experience, two of them were computer-wise and
three had been cashiers. What more do they want?"

Marcy envisioned Gail pushing back a strand of
gray hair. "You know the answer to that as well as I
do. They want the cheapest they can get . . . someone
who'll work overtime without pay, like you do, and
devote their life to the company."

"They'll never find anyone," Marcy groaned. "I'm
doomed."

"Well, cheer up, honey, and I'll see what I can do.
They have a new girl in personnel who's not only gorgeous but brilliant. I'll get to work on her right away."

"Thanks, Gail. Just knowing I have someone on my
team makes me feel better already."

They talked for a few minutes, then rang off. Marcy
sat back for a moment, absently tapping her pen on
the desk. Her office was very small and crowded with
the computer console and office register along one
wall and a second desk wedged between two filing
cabinets. The desk, unused now, was cluttered with
papers and boxes and operational-procedure manuals.

Marcy's eyes strayed to the empty desk chair and
stayed there for a long, pensive moment. Then,
almost without realizing what she was doing, she
reached for the yellow pages of the Fort Lauderdale
phone book and turned to the section headed
"Accountants." She ran her finger down the column
of certified public accountants . . . and there it was.
Drew W. Bradford. So, he really was an accountant,
she mused. Beginning at the top of the list again, she
started checking the listings by phone number. It
didn't take long. Collins and Collins on Broward had
the same address and phone number. Evidently he

was in a firm of accountants, but not a partner. She replaced the yellow pages on the phone stand and opened up the residential section. There was only one D. W. Bradford listed. It was on Hillshire Drive . . . very plush, very exclusive, and a long way from the Super S. Had he moved from there recently? Someplace closer, perhaps?

Slowly Marcy closed the book, her brow furrowed as unanswered questions spun through her head. Who was this Drew Bradford, this enigma of a man whose face was etched so clearly in her mind? She could still see him leaning casually against the doorjamb, his eyes gently amused, his lips parted slightly in a provocative smile, his voice low with an underlying sensuality that made Marcy's breath catch in her throat. Even now she could feel the warm strength of his hand as it held hers in a viselike grip, as though reluctant to release her. Suddenly Marcy felt a shiver race down her spine and sat up abruptly. This was no time to be daydreaming. Drew Bradford was obviously a playboy, a beach bum who could afford not to take his job too seriously. He seemed to have a lot of free time, which he idled away by playing games. Marcy couldn't understand why applying for jobs, which he was obviously overqualified for, turned him on, but she wasn't a psychologist or a dreamer. She was a hardworking store manager who had two hours of data to process before she went home. And if she didn't get to it, she reminded herself sternly, she'd be here all night.

With one quick movement, she shoved her chair back and stood up, determined to put Drew Bradford out of her thoughts. Straightening her blue regulation lab coat, she walked over to the computer, smoothing the folds of the jacket in place. She looked down at herself and the colorless shapeless uniform.

She tried smoothing it down over her stomach, but it puckered up again, bringing a frown to her face. God, this is ugly, she thought. And then a smile tipped the corners of her mouth. At least Drew had been right about one thing. . . .

Tuesday was the quietest day of the week for Marcy, and she looked forward to it with an almost childlike anticipation. Since she didn't have to go in to work until ten, she had time for forty-five minutes of jazzercise before she showered and dressed. She had several exercise tapes that she used to follow routinely, but since moving to Fort Lauderdale, she hadn't had the time or the energy to devote to the muscle tones of her body. Usually when she got home at night it was all she could do to cook a simple dinner before falling into bed. But on Tuesdays, she did her hair and her nails and dawdled over her coffee before driving the one mile from her apartment to the store.

Since this was also catch-up day, she cleaned off her desk, sorting papers and filing away forms and letters, getting ready to start her weekly report. She was just beginning column one when Louella tapped lightly on the open door.

"Cindy's not coming in today. She has the flu or something."

"Hmm. How many cashiers does that leave us?"

"Four."

Marcy thought a moment. "Well, that's a little short. We might be able to get by, but I don't want to take a chance. I'll call Roberta and see if she can come in at noon."

"Right," Louella answered as she went back to her station.

Marcy dialed Roberta's number, but didn't get an answer. She tried the name of the next cashier on the list and got a busy signal. She was going down the roster, her head bent over the book, when she had the strangest feeling that the air around her was being electrically charged. She looked up, startled, just as Drew Bradford strode into the room.

He was grinning with an overflow of well-being, the picture of the young, aggressive executive who's just gotten a big promotion. He was dressed in pale yellow summer slacks and an open-collared white shirt. He seemed to be very pleased with himself, pleased with his surroundings, pleased with life. Marcy couldn't help but smile. His nature was as sunny as his looks.

He cast Marcy the most devastating smile she'd ever seen. "It's good to see you again, Marcy."

Her heart melted at the lingering ring of his words, the huskiness of his voice, the way that voice made her name sound like a caress. . . .

"I know we'll get along just great." He smiled.

Yesss, she thought, drinking in his vitality, we should . . .

He put the paper bag he was carrying down on the other desk. "Is this mine?" he asked.

She looked puzzled. Was he talking about the brown paper bag, she wondered?

Without waiting for an answer, he scooped all the papers and catalogs off the desk, put them on top of the file cabinet and pulled the desk chair back to open the top drawer.

"Hmmm. This'll be fine." He nodded and, delving into the paper bag, brought out a glass paperweight, a pencil caddy, two books and a little triangular desk sign with his name on it. He turned it so it would face Marcy. "In case you forget," he joshed.

"Forget?" What did that mean?

"I have more stuff in my car, but I'll get that later."

"Later?" She didn't understand.

"Right now, I know you want to get started."

"Started?" For the life of her, she didn't know what was going on. "I hate to sound like an echo, but what the hell *is* all this stuff?" She got up with an impatient gesture and walked over to the desk. After examining the contents with a critical squint, she turned her gaze to Drew. "If you're looking for the flea market, it's down the street a mile."

He dropped a handful of pens, pencils, rubber bands and paper clips into the drawer. "These are my tools of the trade," he explained. "I can't work without them."

But Marcy still didn't understand. "Well, what are you bringing them here for? You can't clutter up this desk like that."

"What do you mean clutter up? It's *my* desk."

"*Your* desk?" Was there something wrong with her hearing?

"Certainly. Didn't you get your notice? I'm the new assistant manager."

Marcy blinked, feeling absolutely stunned. She simply stood there and stared, openmouthed and vacant-eyed. "Assistant manager?" she repeated, hardly believing her own voice. "Notice?"

It was Drew's turn to look surprised, or at least he appeared to look surprised. Marcy wasn't quite sure. . . .

"Didn't anyone tell you I'd been hired on as your new assistant manager?" His eyes were round, questioning, innocent, yet somehow Marcy had the feeling he was testing her.

"No, they didn't," she stated firmly. She could feel her anger rapidly rising to the surface. Did this egomaniac standing before her really think he could get away with a coup like this? "I don't know where you get your wild ideas, Mr. Bradford, but I find them very hard to swallow. The last time I saw you, which was less than a week ago, you hadn't even applied for the job." She stood back, arms crossed in a gesture of defiance. Now if she could just keep her breathing under control . . .

"Ahh," he said, raising a calming hand. "That's where I took your advice."

"I didn't know I'd given any."

He gave her an appealing smile. "Yes, inadvertently, you did. You made me realize that job applications aren't exactly cherished by the company. So I drove over to Tampa myself and wrangled an interview with the new personnel director."

Marcy lifted a suspicious brow. "The new one? The good-looking one?"

He couldn't control a sly grin. "She was very charming."

"And so were you, I'm sure."

"Well, I *was* on my best behavior that day."

"I'll bet you were."

Drew inclined his head in a nod of thanks and walked around the desk to stand directly in front of her. Marcy had the feeling that she should move back to give him more room, give *her* more room, put some distance between them. His nearness had a way of upsetting her balance and this was no time to lose control. He had blatantly overstepped her authority, and if she didn't put her foot down now, she was lost.

She swung away from him and marched back to her desk. While her back was still to him, Marcy took a deep breath and pulled her face into her pragmatic, business-as-usual expression. Though Marcy's body was throbbing with mixed emotions, she had no intention of succumbing to the magnetism of his charisma. Still, she was grateful to have the solid bulk of her desk between them.

"As I mentioned to you before," she explained carefully, "the personnel director does *only* the initial screening of the applicants. The store managers make the final decisions. I'm afraid your friend has overstepped her authority, and I have no intentions of standing idly by and letting her get away with it."

To Marcy's amazement, Drew nodded in complete agreement. "I wouldn't take it either if I were you," he stated flatly. "Just look at the embarrassing position it's put us both in. Here I am all set to go to work on this data processing"—he indicated the computer— "and I find myself involved in a typical company snafu. If I were you, I'd file a formal complaint so fast, it'd make your head swim."

Marcy nodded, surprised at his anger, and beginning to wonder if perhaps the error wasn't his fault after all. It could be that the new girl simply wanted to impress Drew Bradford and took it upon herself to hire him. Marcy could understand this, but she had no intention of tolerating it. That bright-eyed bunny in personnel had just better read her manual again!

Marcy picked up the company phone directory. "I'll call in right now!" she stormed.

Drew sauntered over to her desk, his face drawn into a thoughtful frown. "I wouldn't telephone," he advised. "I think it's too important for that. A manager and a customer are involved here. When you phone, you never know who's going to relay your message or how they're going to reword your complaint." He sat down on the edge of her desk and folded his arms loosely in front of him. His voice dropped to a low, conspiratorial tone. "If I were you, I'd file a formal complaint."

"You would?" She'd never done that before. . . .

"Absolutely." Drew leaned forward a little. Marcy leaned back. "The written word always carries more weight than the spoken one. It reaches more people. And no one can misinterpret your words for you . . . it's right there in black and white. It demands a response."

Marcy nodded, agreeing. "I've never sent in a written report before, but we have a form here." She started rummaging through a desk drawer. "The response couldn't be any worse than what I've been getting." She pulled out a thin manual. "Here it is. If I get it in the mail today, they should have it by tomorrow."

"I would think so."

Marcy raised her eyes to his. "I'm glad you suggested this." She smiled warmly. "I might even send it to the vice-president. He's very concerned about all aspects of the business."

"Fine," he said, but his voice didn't have that final ring to it, indicating the subject was closed. Marcy looked up, perplexed. He was studying her as though he wanted to say something but was hesitant to do so. He frowned slightly and cleared his throat. "We have to keep in mind," he cautioned, "that there's always the possibility we could be wrong."

She sat up. "What do you mean?"

Drew slid his long arm across her desk and leaned into it. Their faces were so close she could almost feel his breath on her cheek. "I'm sure you're aware of how Super S is changing procedures and streamlining operations all the time in order to keep the company right up there in a highly competitive position."

"Yes, of course," she murmured vaguely.

"They'd have to, to survive," he said, as though reminding her of the importance of the situation. "Which means that there's a possibility you could be wrong about the employment regulations."

"Oh, no. Never."

"Well, now, think about it," he cautioned. "It seems to me there's been a shake-up recently in personnel. Of course, this is just my own observation, but if I were you, I think I'd check into the regulations before I wrote this letter of formal complaint. There's a slim possibility you could be wrong, and it would put us both in a bad light."

"How do you figure that?"

"Well," he hurried on, very smoothly, she noticed, "it would appear that you were rejecting personnel's decision, or that I failed to show up for work."

Marcy paused, thoughtfully. There was the barest possibility he could be right. "There *is* a new manual out," she murmured half to herself, "but I haven't gotten mine yet. I just assumed it was the same as the last one."

His voice was grave. "I wouldn't take a chance. Get the book first and make sure you're right."

He straightened, stretching his arms back a little as if to relieve an ache in his shoulders. It was a natural gesture, but Marcy had the uncomfortable feeling that it was more for her benefit than his. She realized how right she was when Drew got to his feet.

"In the meantime"—he sighed gustily—"I suppose I'll have to stay on the job."

Marcy lifted a suspicious brow. "Don't put yourself out. I'm sure if there's been some error, they'll understand."

He looked at her with an expression of disbelief. "How could you be so unprofessional? With the possibility of new regulations staring you right in the face, you stubbornly refuse to acknowledge them!"

"Don't tell me who's stubborn!" she flared. "You're not even legally employed. Besides, what do you know about the supermarket business? All you CPA's know is tax work."

His glance sharpened instantly. She could see the corners of his mouth curve upward. "How did you know I was a CPA?"

"I looked it up in the phone book," she admitted, not at all embarrassed at her actions. "I also noticed you were with the firm of Collins and Collins." It was her turn to lean forward on the desk in an aggressive pose. "So perhaps you'd like to explain why you're applying for the job of assistant manager."

If she thought he was going to back down, she was very much mistaken. Resting his hands on the desk, Drew leaned toward her until their faces were inches apart. But despite the growing feeling of awareness coursing through her, Marcy stubbornly refused to back off.

His words were flat and evenly spaced. "The firm of Collins and Collins happens to consist of my ex-brother-in-law and my ex-father-in-law. Now, you tell me how you'd like to work with your ex-in-laws. . . ."

"I wouldn't," she conceded.

"I was the bright young boy who married the boss's daughter. We were divorced last summer. I was ready to leave then, but that would have put them in a bind. I had no quarrel with my in-laws, though I wanted to get as far away from Adele as possible; so I agreed to stay until May first when the tax season was over."

Marcy found herself inadvertently pulling away from him a little. He seemed to be getting closer all the time. "I see," she said, drawing herself up straight. There was something boldly intimidating about his nearness. It made her breath come in short gasps. "So you've been unemployed since May first . . ."

"Yes," he said without hesitation.

She shook her head. "I don't think you're going to be satisfied in this job. You're overqualified."

Drew stood up then and put his hands back in his pockets. "I have two friends who are also accountants. We're going to open up our own practice in October." He threw his hands out in an empty gesture. "So until then, I have nothing to do."

Marcy's face clouded with indignation. "If you think I'm going to waste my time training you when you're only going to be here three months, you're crazy!"

"Ah, ah, ah," he cautioned, raising a restraining hand. "Remember, I was hired by the main office. . . ." His words trailed off meaningfully, but the disarming smile on his face never wavered. She started to protest but couldn't rally quick enough before her glance caught the figure of Louella in the doorway. Marcy motioned her into the room.

"I hate to interrupt"—Louella sighed heavily—"but those bag boys are fooling around in the parking lot again, and—"

Marcy was on her feet before Louella finished the sentence. "I'll fix them," she stated grimly as she started out the door.

Louella stood a little to one side to let her pass. It was then that Marcy realized that Louella's face was a ghastly shade of gray. She stopped in midstride. "What's the matter, Louella? Are you all right?"

The older woman shook her head. "I hate to tell you, Marcy, what with Cindy off and all, but I think I'm getting the flu, too. I feel terrible."

Marcy put her arm around Louella's shoulder and turned her toward the door. "You look terrible, too. Go back to the break room and lie down. I'll straighten out these kids in the lot and be with you in a minute."

"Why don't you go back with Louella," Drew suggested, "and let me handle the bag boys?"

Marcy hesitated, undecided. She didn't want Drew Bradford to get the idea that she was going to hire him. But they *were* one cashier short, and now with Louella out, all she could do was pray for a slow day. If the customers had to queue up to check out, they'd be furious and—oh, hell, she thought, he was better than nothing.

Finally, she nodded her consent. "All right, but don't be too easy on those kids. They've been doing this for a week now."

The satisfied look of triumph in his face was almost unbearable, but what could she do? Marcy watched his tall, muscle-toned body bound out of the office and through the store. Despite his teasing way, Marcy knew that all the problems with the bag boys would be solved immediately and permanently. There was something about Drew Bradford that demanded obedience.

Marcy heard Louella exhale a long, dreamy sigh. "Is he the new assistant manager?" she whispered hopefully.

"No, of course not," Marcy said crisply. "He's just here for today."

"Too bad." Louella sighed, running her tongue across her parched lips. "If he was here, no one would ever get sick. . . ."

# Chapter Three

❧

Marcy called Louella's daughter, who said she'd be right over. Then she helped Louella to the break room and settled her on the cot that was standard equipment in all Super S break rooms, as were the metal tables and chairs, the four vending machines, the microwave oven, refrigerator, sink and cupboards where employees stored their lunches. It was a utilitarian room, devoid of any personality, comfortable enough for short breaks but not a place where one would want to linger too long.

Once satisfied that she'd done all she could for Louella, Marcy went back to her office. As she passed through the stockroom Mr. Morton, the manager of groceries, stopped her. He'd just hung up the phone.

"That was the home office," he said, thoroughly discouraged. "They said the supply truck has broken down on the freeway and will be about four hours late." He threw his hands up in a gesture of hopelessness. "So here I sit with a full stock crew and nothing for them to do. The truck will probably get here after they go home. What do you want me to do? Should I have them unhitch the trailer and leave it here all night? We can unload it in the morning."

Marcy shook her head, frowning. That had been done many times before, but it was becoming increasingly more dangerous. They were all aware of the incident at the Super S in Orlando. The trailer had been backed up to the receiving door and unhitched from the tractor, to be unloaded the next day. During the night, someone had backed a tractor up to the trailer, hitched up and driven off, never to be seen again. Marcy had talked to the manager of the Orlando store later, and he told her that the loss had been charged to his store, making his margin of profit the lowest in the chain. And if there was one thing Marcy didn't need right now, she decided, it was to be at the bottom of the net profit range.

She looked at her watch. "Well, if they're here by two, and the boys don't leave until four, and if I loan you a bag boy . . ." Her voice trailed off. It still wouldn't give them enough time. Her thoughts immediately shifted to Drew. As much as she hated to use him, she was in a bind. With his accounting background, Mr. Morton could teach him how to slot in a few minutes. With enough help, they could finish the unloading in three hours.

"Let me think about it, Mr. Morton, and I'll get back to you."

"I'll be here," he said, grimly.

Marcy pushed through the swinging doors and started for her office, changed her mind and went down aisle seven this time. She picked up a dozen eggs someone had left on top of the canned pineapple and returned them to the dairy department. As she passed the cashiers she noticed that there were no customers in line and that all bag boys were not only on duty but moving with more speed than she'd ever seen.

"Can I help you, ma'am?" came a voice from above her. She raised her eyes to Louella's elevated station and was met by Drew's infectious smile.

"What are you doing up there?" she asked.

His smile never wavered. "The cashiers tell me

they're ready to take their lunch breaks and have to check out their drawers. That's Louella's job, isn't it?"

"Yes, but they don't have to ring out until they're through for the day. Just tell them to bring their trays into the office until after their break. Then I want to see you."

He nodded, then turned his attention to a customer who was complaining because they didn't carry Eaglewing cigarettes. He handled the situation by turning on the charm that Marcy knew would melt the woman's heart. With a shake of her head, Marcy went into the office and called one of the cashiers to come in early. She'd just hung up the phone when Drew came in. She could see now that he was wearing the regulation blue blazer with the big gold Super S on the pocket. She had to admit it had never looked so good on anyone before. It made Marcy even more conscious of his broad shoulders and his tall, athletic body.

"Where did you get that?" she asked.

"Someone in produce loaned it to me." He eyed her levelly. "I take it I'm supposed to order one of my own?"

"I wouldn't rush it if I were you," she advised.

Though her words were stern, her head swirled with confusion. Before she wrote her letter of formal complaint, Marcy wanted to call Gail to make sure the rules really had been changed. Surprisingly, she almost hoped that they had. She could never hire anyone, knowing they'd only be there three months, but if that responsibility had been taken out of her hands, what could she do? She'd have to accept this handsome man standing before her, wouldn't she? But what if the rules hadn't been changed? Then what would she do? She paused thoughtfully, torn between her loyalty to the company and her own desperate need for an assistant—even if it was only for a little while.

He was still watching her, those blue eyes never wavering. The corners of his mouth were tilted slightly in a maddening look of amusement, as though he knew something she didn't. It was almost like a provocative invitation, so appealing, so irresistible, so . . .

Marcy yanked open a desk drawer and withdrew the size charts for employee uniforms. She hesitated a moment before she handed them to him. "You can look at these, I suppose, but don't order one."

Drew reached out to take the charts, but he merely grasped them, he didn't pull them out of her hand. Marcy looked up questioningly, and for several unnerving moments, she felt an intense physical awareness of him. Somehow, she knew that he was experiencing the same sensation. But where Marcy tried to conceal it, Drew faced it boldly, as if challenging its existence. He kept studying her face, searching her eyes with a gentle, intimate look, as tender as a caress. She tried to keep her features expressionless, but despite his arrogance and unflappable self-confidence, she was finding his charm hard to resist. And there was something else about him: an intensity, an inner strength that he apparently kept on a tight rein. Instinctively, Marcy knew that behind his easy banter and winning smile was a wiry toughness that would be very difficult to conquer . . . not that she'd want to.

She lowered her eyes to her desk and busied herself by rearranging her pencils with one hand until the lump in her throat dissolved.

"When the time comes to order," she said, managing to put a crisp businesslike note into her voice, "the company will pay half the cost. The other half comes out of the employee's salary."

Drew grinned and she knew he was aware of her fight to recapture her composure. "In that case," he said, slowly pulling the charts out of her hand, "I shall order very prudently."

Shifting his gaze to the chart, he started reading. Marcy welcomed the silence that fell between them. She needed a moment or two to catch her breath. Unfortunately, the respite didn't last long.

Drew pointed to the charts. Marcy noticed he was on the women's page. "Do you mean to say you women have a choice? That you can either wear a lab coat or a blazer?"

"That's right."

He looked at her, incredulous. "And you chose the lab coat?"

"Certainly," she said, looking down at the shapeless garment. "It covers more of your clothing and is, therefore, more protective."

"To hell with the protection. No one with your shape should try to hide it. You're doing your co-workers a disservice."

She straightened defensively. "What do you know about my shape? There's always the possibility that the lab coat is an improvement over what lies beneath it."

"Oh, no." He smiled and rakishly wagged his finger at her. "I saw you in the parking lot one day when you were leaving. You were wearing a full skirt and when you bent over to put something on the floor of the backseat, the wind caught your skirt and blew it up to your waist. I saw a terrific pair of legs . . . shapely, suntanned, well toned—"

"I wasn't aware I was being watched." She tried to sound indignant, but her words lacked the sting they needed to be convincing. Marcy knew he was just teasing, but something feminine inside her responded to his compliment, sending a warm glow flowing through her. Drew Bradford's charm was proving to be more compelling than she cared to admit.

The sudden ring of the phone jangled her back to reality. Drew reached for it, but Marcy grabbed it first.

She flashed him a condescending smile. "I can manage," she informed him, grateful for the interruption as well as the chance to remind herself that theirs was a business relationship only. There was nothing personal between them, and it was going to stay that way.

The call was from the main office, assuring her that the truck had been repaired and was on the way.

"Mr. Morton will be glad to hear that." She sighed, then, as an afterthought, added, "Put me through to Gail Stromberg, will you?" She lifted her eyes to Drew. "We might as well get this settled here and now."

"I'm sorry," came the operator's whiny voice, "but that line is busy."

"Oh, all right, I'll call back later."

As she hung up Marcy took a deep breath and raised her eyes to her temporary assistant. Drew had an intriguing way of appearing to be waiting patiently while still emanating restlessness. It was very disconcerting.

"Well"—she sighed resignedly—"I'm still not sure you're supposed to be here, but I'm so desperate I'm going to use you anyway. You can help Mr. Morton. I don't know what else to do with you."

"Are you asking for suggestions?" Obviously he was full of them.

"No, I'm not," she retorted, but didn't get to continue. She could hear the distinctive throb of the Security Division armored truck pulling up to the front of the store. "Oh, damn," she complained, "you never know when they're coming to get the money."

"That's the point," Drew said, starting for the door. He gave her a saluting wave. "See you later?"

"I suppose." She shrugged. And then she smiled. As far as assistants went, she could do worse.

Marcy nodded a greeting to the driver of the armored truck as he came into her office. Out of habit he closed the door behind him and snapped the lock. This seemed like a futile gesture since almost everyone who worked at the Super S knew where the safe was, but there was always the possibility that a customer would stray into the office at the wrong time and find Marcy and the guard on their hands and knees. All Super S Markets had a floor safe. Inside this was a drop box. Marcy opened the combination lock, then stood back to let the guard open the second lock with his key. Together they removed the envelopes, each containing one thousand dollars, counted them and put them into a canvas bag that was then tied and sealed with crimping pliers. Receipts were exchanged and, within minutes, the guard was out of the office, in the truck and back onto the boulevard. Less than five minutes had elapsed from the time he walked in until the time he left.

As usual, Marcy sighed with relief when she heard the armored truck pull away from the building. She was never afraid of being held up in terms of her own safety, but the loss of one deposit would be charged against the store, thus reducing her profit picture. That could be fatal for a new manager, and Marcy was still more or less on probation. Though no one had come right out and said so, it was apparent from the continual checkups by the home office that someone up there doubted her ability. Marcy could understand this. Just because she'd worked in the main office nine years didn't necessarily qualify her for a position as a store manager. Though they always promoted from within, her promotion had been an exception, as was Drew's. Strange, she thought, that they'd put two inexperienced managers into the same store. Well, she rationalized, that was the way of big business. In their effort to streamline operations, they depended on computers instead of common sense.

Since there was no other emergency for over two hours, Marcy was able to concentrate on her weekly report. She was just finishing it up when the day book-keeper put her head in the doorway.

"Do you want me to work in the computer room or take Louella's station until the next shift comes on?"

"Take Louella's station, Karen. I need you up front. I have to go back to see how the unloading is coming."

If Karen looked surprised, Marcy didn't notice. It seemed perfectly normal for the store manager to want to check up on the weekly delivery from the main warehouse. The fact that she hadn't done this once in the two months she'd been there left Karen gaping, but Marcy was unaware of it as she swept out of the office.

A conveyor belt extended from the bed of the trailer into the receiving room. Cases of merchandise moved down the belt with amazing speed. Drew was standing to one side with a clipboard in his hand, checking off each piece against the master sheet. He had one foot on the floor and the other on top of a wooden packing case. Marcy couldn't help but notice that he looked very much at ease, unhurried, unruf-fled, in complete control. It was hot in the room and Drew, like everyone else, had removed his jacket. Tiny beads of perspiration dotted his forehead, but a swath of wheat-colored hair fell forward a little, sug-gesting a casualness that negated any hint of discomfort. Marcy wondered if he was this sure of himself in everything he did.

Not wanting to interrupt, Marcy started for the break room, but was sidetracked by Mr. Morton, who seemed anxious to talk to her. He shouted a few instructions to the boys who were loading the boxes on uni-carts, then, turning his back to them, he leaned toward Marcy and dropped his voice to a low, conspiratorial whisper.

"Jeez, that guy's fast. I tell ya. He learned to slot off in ten minutes. And now he's better than I am." He motioned to the trailer. "I got three guys in there unloading as fast as they can. We'll be through here in a half hour." He scratched his head. "Never seen anything like it."

Marcy felt a sense of pride welling within her. Why, she didn't know. She wasn't responsible for his being there. "I'm glad he's working out," she said, deliberately leaving the impression that it was all her doing.

But Mr. Morton had something else on his mind. He cast Marcy a quick glance. "Is he gonna stay long?"

"I hope so," she said with a brief nod and started edging toward the break room so Mr. Morton wouldn't see the guilt in her face.

Why can't anything be easy for me? she asked herself. Why does everything have to have so many complications? Drew had been on the job one day and already he'd whipped the bag boys into shape, learned how to check out the cashiers' drawers and now he was slotting off like an old pro. No wonder Mr. Morton couldn't believe this boon of good fortune. She could hardly believe it herself.

Marcy started to pour herself a cup of coffee, but the pot was almost empty. Rinsing it out, she refilled it, a chore they all shared, but she decided against waiting for it. She always kept tomato juice on ice, but when she opened the refrigerator door and reached for it, her hand stopped in midmotion. Someone had put a bottle of wine in there to cool. This was a blatant violation of the company rules; employees weren't allowed to keep alcoholic beverages on the premises. If they wanted to buy wine or beer they had to do so *after* they punched out for the day. She removed the bottle, unscrewed the cap and was just ready to pour it down the sink when she heard Drew's voice behind her.

"Oh? Aren't we a little early for cocktails? Not that I'm against it, you understand." He came right up behind her and took the bottle out of her hand. "Glasses?"

"I should have guessed it was yours," she said. "There's a strict company rule against keeping alcoholic beverages in the break room."

She wanted to drive her point home by drilling him with her most condemning stare, but she couldn't turn around. He was standing too close. If she turned to face him, they'd be practically cheek to cheek, a position her nerve center told her to avoid. She didn't know Drew Bradford very well, but she was quite sure he'd never back up a step to relieve her discomfort. In fact, Marcy thought, recalling the aggressive way he had stretched his arm across her desk, it was just possible he'd lean closer.

"Even if the bottle's sealed?" he asked, his breath very close to her hair.

She nodded once. "Even if it's sealed," she stated flatly. She was beginning to feel terribly inadequate, standing there facing the wall.

"And what if it's unsealed?"

Marcy realized he was stalling and had no intention of stepping back or releasing her until she made the first move. Damn his arrogance, she thought, and pivoted a half turn. Sliding against the sink, she stepped to one side, but her hip bumped against him slightly. His response was a satisfied grin followed by a critical perusal of her body.

"That lab coat has to go."

Clapping a hand to her waist, Marcy shot him a withering look. "We weren't discussing lab coats. We were discussing the possession of wine on the premises."

He cast a glance over his shoulder as though to make sure no one was there. "Believe me, Marcy. Your secret is safe with me."

"This is *not* mine and you know it!" she retorted. "I assumed it was yours."

"No, I stick to beer and before-dinner cocktails. Which reminds me," he said, glancing at his watch, "it's about that time."

Before Marcy could blink, he reached out, took her arm and started for the door. "We *are* going to celebrate our first day of working together, aren't we?" His grip tightened.

It was a raw act of possession, and Marcy's whole body became intensely aware of his nearness. She had to take a breath before she could speak.

"I don't think seeing each other outside of business hours is a good idea," she said, freeing her arm. "Something tells me it's going to take all the tolerance we can muster just to get through our jobs on a daily basis."

If Marcy thought she was putting him down, she was mistaken. With an expressive lift of his shoulders, Drew admitted the possibility had merits. But the glint of indulgent humor in his eyes told her he wasn't buying it.

A stirring just outside the door jarred Marcy back to

the present. Drew turned her toward the sink and gave her an affectionate pat on the arm.

"Better get rid of the evidence." He winked suggestively. Then, in four long strides, he was through the door and out of sight.

Marcy completed her last sit-up and lay flat on her back on the floor of her air-conditioned living room, relaxing. She was a firm believer in the theory that exercise could empty the mind of all anxieties of the day, and usually it did. But this time she found her thoughts continually drifting back to Drew Bradford.

As she stared at the ceiling she tried to gather random impressions of him and shape them into a personality she could comprehend, but he didn't seem to fit into any mold she was familiar with. That disturbed her. It made her feel as though she'd stumbled onto something she didn't understand, and Marcy was a person who liked everything carefully spelled out, categorized, tagged, registered. She realized this was almost an obsession with her and worried sometimes that she might develop into a walking computer. But she couldn't help it, that was her way. And that was why Drew was continually in her thoughts.

Stretching her arms over her head, she bent her knees, put her feet flat on the floor and let her mind drift. He was fun to be with, she thought dreamily. He was tough-minded yet obviously enjoyed the good life. He had a lot of control and a comfortable way of handling himself, but there was also something shocking about him. He was arrogant and too self-confident for his own good, though she had to admit that he seemed to know just how far to go—at least in his dealings with her. A smile touched the corners of her mouth. It was a strange sensation to realize someone knew how far to pull your strings, but it didn't worry

her. Two could play this game, and Marcy knew the
strategy as well as anyone. In fact, it might even prove
to be interesting, like a contest between two highly
skilled players.

Rolling over onto her side, Marcy got up and
stretched one final time. Then she walked into the
bathroom and turned on the shower. As she waited
for the water to warm up she studied herself in the
full-length mirror. Standing as she was in panties and
bra, the results of her daily exercises were apparent in
her flat stomach, narrow waist, high firm breasts,
straight legs and solid thighs. A commendable figure,
and one that she'd worked hard to attain. Since her
divorce from Roger, she had skimmed off fifteen
pounds of excess fat and had no intention of gaining
it back. She turned sideways for a profile view. Not
bad. Maybe Drew was right. Maybe it was time to
shuck the lab coat. She had a few straight skirts hanging in her closet as well as a regulation blue blazer.
Maybe tomorrow she would wear them. . . .

As she stepped into the shower Marcy realized that
her spirits were higher than they'd been in a long
time. She wasn't fooling herself, though. She knew
very well that she would be dressing for Drew, and
while one part of her hated to admit he had so much
influence on her, the other part said, so what? It
wasn't as though she was a giddy teenager who didn't
know what was going on. Drew was a very attractive
man whom she found interesting and appealing—a
perfectly normal reaction for a perfectly normal
single woman.

As the strong nettles of the spray cascaded down
her back she turned slowly, rinsing the soap off her
body. Then she shut off the water and stepped out of
the stall. Reaching for a towel and starting to dry herself, Marcy could see tiny blond hairs shimmering like

gold against her suntanned arms and she realized how very much alike in coloring she and Drew were. Though he had blue eyes and she had brown, their hair was about the same shade and they both sported a deep bronzed tan. She wondered where he'd gotten his. At the beach? She'd never seen him there. Did he live in an apartment where they had a pool? Did he go fishing? Have a boat? Oh, hell, she thought, tossing the towel onto a hook, why was she letting him walk all over her mind like this? If she wanted to know more about him, she shouldn't have refused to have a drink with him after work.

Make up your mind, Marcy, she chastised herself. Admit that he's interesting and that you want to know more about him. Despite a rather shaky introductory period, he was probably Mr. Average Guy who didn't have a conniving bone in his body. Straightforward, honest, forthright, hardworking . . . the list went on and on even as she closed her eyes in sleep.

Marcy sat at her desk the next morning, absolutely motionless. She reread the letter twice before shock gave way to reality. The hiring procedures for the Super S hadn't been changed. In fact, the form she held in her hand was the same one they'd been using for ten years. The same words of explanation were there: the manager of the store was to interview the following applicants and hire the one best suited to his or her needs. Beneath that was a space where the names and addresses of four applicants were alphabetically listed in a neatly typed row. Drew's name was one of the four.

As Marcy lowered the paper to her desk she dropped her head into her hands and bit back a wave of anger. Drew had deliberately tricked her into believing that the employment rules had been

changed and that the home office was making all the
decisions. Blindly, she'd let him influence her. She'd
believed him. She'd let him walk in here—no, not walk
in, *move* in—and convince her with his wide-eyed
innocence that there had been a mistake of some kind.
The oldest story in the world, and she'd fallen for it.

Of course, now that she had the advantage of hind-
sight, she could see exactly what had happened. He'd
gone to Tampa, charmed the new woman in personnel into going out to lunch with him and then proceeded to wangle a promise out of her to put his name
on the list. In her position, that would have been easy
to do. But hire him? No. Marcy should have realized
that a change in company policy as drastic as that
would have required months of lengthy discussions
before it was implemented.

She'd foolishly ignored the inner warning signals
she'd felt the day she met him. She knew then that he
was aggressive and pushy and determined to have his
way. Well, she thought, there was no sense in crying
about it now. Fortunately, no damage had been done
except to her pride, and that would heal in time. She
picked up a pencil and tapped it against her teeth.
Why was it that planning revenge always seemed to
shorten the time span?

Drew waltzed in less than thirty minutes later looking magnificent in a blue sport shirt that matched his
eyes. He smiled and started to greet her, but stopped
when he saw the look on Marcy's face. He knew
instantly what was wrong, but his reaction wasn't what
Marcy had expected. Instead of being chagrined, he
was maddeningly unconcerned. Not only that, he
seemed to find Marcy's displeasure very amusing, a
reaction that sent her temper soaring. If he thought
for one minute he was going to manipulate her again,
he was mistaken.

Looking him squarely in the eyes, she tossed the brown paper bag across the desk. "Start packing," she gritted through clenched teeth.

His face creased into a sudden smile. He just stood there, shaking his head in a condescending way. "Now, what is it today?" he chided. "Another crisis? Must I be consulted about every little thing that comes up?"

"You know very well what I'm talking about," she blazed with mounting rage. "You deliberately led me to believe that you'd been hired by the main office. You even encouraged me to write a letter to complain about failing to notify the managers about the change in rules. That was a very clever ploy. Thank God it didn't work."

"Why didn't it work?" he challenged. "Why didn't you write that letter? Or phone them again?" He moved toward her desk.

"I never dreamed you could be so deceitful!"

"No, that's not why." He leaned his hands on her desk. "You wanted me to stay, but you didn't want the responsibility of hiring me, knowing I'd only be here a few months. It was much easier to let someone else make that decision."

"That's not true at all!" she retorted, jumping to her feet. "How dare you accuse me of shirking my duties?"

"I didn't mean shirking. I meant shifting. And there's nothing wrong with that as long as the company gains from it. All businesses do it."

She picked up the list of applicants. "And what about these people? Do you think it's fair to bypass them in favor of someone who slid in via the back door?"

He shrugged, unconcerned. "Look, they all had the

same opportunities. Any one of them could have done what I did if they'd wanted the job bad enough."

"They wouldn't think of doing such a despicable thing. They're good, upright citizens. They handed their applications into the Super S because they had faith in the fairness of their company. They trusted us." She slammed the paper down on the desk. "And, damn it, I'm not going to let them down. I'm going to call each one of them in for an interview and select the one most suited for the job."

"Good idea. I couldn't agree more." Pulling a chair up to her desk, he sat down, his feet spread apart, his forearms resting on his knees. He seemed to be taking up an awful lot of room. . . .

"What do you think you're doing?"

"I'm waiting for my interview. My name's on that list, too, remember? I demand equal time."

"Oh, all right!" She yanked her chair out and sat down heavily, her brow creased with annoyance. Extracting the application tablet from a drawer, she picked up her pen and put the date at the top of the page.

He leaned toward her, dangerously close. "I already filled one of those out, remember?"

"You may have filled one out in Tampa, but I don't have a copy of it here," she replied. "How can I make a decision without comparing the applications?"

"I was under the impression that you were going to make the decision on the basis of your personal interviews."

"I am," she snapped, "but this comes first."

Marcy realized she was sounding childish, but it was hard to balance her anger with her sense of fairness and the drugging magnetism of Drew's nearness. He was sitting so close she could feel the heat of his body, smell the crisp scent of his after-shave . . . She caught herself suddenly and managed to get herself under control despite the amused lift of his brow and the lazily seductive look he gave her.

She picked up her pen. "I need your name. Last name first. Then first name. Then middle initial. And spell it out, please."

She saw his gaze take in her freshly ironed blazer and tight skirt. Why, today of all days, had she decided to change her uniform? she asked herself. Would she never learn?

The pen was poised. "Last name?" she said.

"B-R-A-D-F-O-R-D." He spelled it out slowly.

"First name?"

"D-R-E-W."

"Middle initial?"

"W. D-O-U-B-L-E dash U."

Marcy's pen stopped moving. Without raising her head, she glared up at him from beneath her long lashes. "Mr. Bradford," she began, very patiently.

"I thought we'd decided on Drew and Marcy."

"That was yesterday."

"What happened between then and now?"

Exasperated, she tossed the pen on her desk and sat back. Slowly she folded her arms across her chest and met his eyes steadily. "Do I have to explain it to you in grammar school English?"

"That might help."

He settled back, ready for the lesson to begin, but Marcy, aware of the teasing glint of humor in his eyes, wasn't going to be sidetracked by his charm this time. She handed him the pen.

"Maybe you'd better fill out your own application," she said curtly. Getting up, she went over to the office register, but before she could even get started on her work, Drew had finished with the application in a few brief strokes. Marcy took a deep, patient breath and

was just ready to launch into her diatribe on the value
of a submitting a neat application when there was a
polite tap on the door. Marcy swung her gaze to
Jason, the young and relatively new manager of produce.

"I hate to interrupt," he apologized, "but some
goon from the Board of Health is poking around in
the coolers, looking for bugs or something on the vegetables."

"Who is he, do you know?" she asked.

"Name's Harrison."

"Oh, damn." She sighed dismally. "He's the worst
pill in the department."

"What's the matter with him?" Drew asked.

"Evidently this is his first job and he's hell-bent on
revolutionizing the entire food industry. He pokes his
nose into everything. He even runs his finger across
the top of the walk-in coolers to make sure there isn't
any dust up there. If there is, he hands us a warning
notice and comes back again in a week or so and we go
through the whole scene again."

Drew nodded. "I know the type . . . a little man with
a little authority becomes a big dragon."

"Exactly," Marcy and Jason chorused in unison.

"I don't like the idea of turning him loose back
there," Jason complained, "but I've got thirty cases of
lettuce to trim and wrap for the sale tomorrow."

Drew got right up. Marcy started to rise, but he
deterred her by placing a large, powerful hand on her
shoulder. "Why don't you stay here and do your inter-
viewing?" he suggested. "I'll handle Mr. Harrison."

Without waiting for her answer, he followed Jason
out of the room. He paused at the door, however, for
one last comment. "We'll save that interview for later
when we won't be interrupted."

Before she could rally with a snappy answer, Drew

was out of sight. She sat down again and propped her hand on her chin. Though she hated to admit it, she had total confidence in Drew's ability to handle Harrison, who, in her opinion, was a sneaky-eyed twenty-year-old know-it-all with an I.Q. of ten. But what could she do? Marcy couldn't throw him out. She couldn't insult him into leaving, and she couldn't reason with him. Well, what the hell, let Drew handle this one, she thought. As long as he was available, she might as well use him.

Marcy's eye fell on Drew's half-finished application. It told her little that she didn't already know and she wondered if this was similar to the application he'd filled out at the home office. He'd listed his previous experience as, simply, "accountant, Collins and Collins." The title CPA had been eliminated. His age was thirty-four, his address was in the same zip area as the store and his marital status was single. The information was rather vague and stereotyped, certainly not distinguishing. It *was* within the realm of possibilities that, without the aid of his friend in personnel, his name would have been submitted anyway, though Marcy doubted that.

The rest of the applicants were people who were already employed by Super S. She recognized the first as the manager of the hardware department in their Plantation store. He'd been there close to ten years. The second was a single woman who was a cashier in the Palm Beach store. The third was a man she'd met in Tampa—nice fellow, intelligent, friendly, dependable and dedicated. He'd make a good assistant manager.

Laying the list out in front of her, she smoothed it out with the heel of her hand. In all fairness, any one of them was a good possibility. Including Drew. Despite his faults, she had to admit that he could take over almost any task and manage to muddle through it somehow. His resourcefulness was unbeatable and, at this point, that was more important to Marcy than experience. Furthermore, he wouldn't have to give two weeks' notice, as did the others, so her relief would be instantaneous—a big, big plus.

It was an easy decision to make and Drew won, hands down. If Marcy felt any twinge of guilt in bypassing the others, she managed to extinguish it by telling herself that Drew would only be at the store three months and the others' chance would come again soon enough. Thus salving her conscience, she faced another problem. How was she going to tell Drew? That his qualifications were superior? Never. That she enjoyed working with him so much that she wouldn't consider anyone else? Fatal. That she'd think about it and let him know later? Better.

As she was filing the forms away for future use Drew suddenly swung into the room. "Where's the operator's instruction book for the cash registers?" he asked, looking around.

"Right there on the shelf." She pointed. "But what happened to Harrison? Did he go?"

"No," he said, thumbing through the book, "but I've delegated that job to Cindy."

Marcy almost lifted out of her chair. "*Cindy?* Our cashier?"

He nodded affirmatively. "I took one look at that guy and realized he'd been handpicked for stupidity. I was just about to freeze into my best smile and approach him when I saw Cindy coming out of the break room. She was wiggling her hefty hips and shaking her curls and batting her eyelashes all over the place, so I took her aside and explained that she was to escort Mr. Harrison through the produce department. We wanted to give her a little break in routine. She thought it was the greatest idea we'd ever had."

"How dare you make such a decision!" Marcy gasped. "Cindy doesn't know the first thing about health inspections!"

"Well . . ." He shrugged. "Neither does Harrison. But they both know body language. If you don't believe me, just watch them. They're in front of the corn-on-the-cob display."

"I don't care *where* they are," she fumed. "You had no right to take Cindy off the register. We're short cashiers as it is."

"Not to worry. I told her I'd take over for her."

"You! What do you know about a register?"

He held up the book. "I'm planning to learn real fast."

Marcy threw her hands up in the air. "That's just great! As if you could learn to work one of those machines in two minutes. And we haven't even gotten into coupons, food stamps, WICs and senior-citizen discounts."

Lowering the book, he pursed his lips in thought. Then, slowly, he raised his eyes to hers and gave her the widest smile he had. "But I'll bet *you* could do it. . . ."

Oh, no, she thought, would it never end? "Certainly I could. Knowing registers is part of my job. But I won't. If you think for one minute I'm going to take over Cindy's job while she does mine—"

"Nonsense. You're relieving her because her register has been coming up short and we want to make sure it isn't her fault. We're doing a test run."

"There's no such a thing."

"Cindy doesn't have to know that."

"The other cashiers will be suspicious."

"Not if we find something wrong."

"How can we do that?"

He placed a reassuring hand on her shoulder for the second time that day. "Leave it to me. I'll not only find something wrong," he promised, "but I'll also be able to repair it."

Marcy raised her eyes heavenward. "I don't know if I can handle this."

He leaned very close and lowered his voice. "Would you rather have Harrison?"

She only needed one moment to make up her mind. "I'll take the register." She sighed resignedly.

# Chapter Four

❦

True to his promise, Drew found something wrong with the cash register and repaired it immediately by reprogramming the cassette. The fact that this could only be done in the home office was never mentioned by the other cashiers, if indeed they even knew. Louella would know, of course, but she wasn't there, and when she returned the following day, evidently no one bothered to mention it. All of the cashiers were so taken with Drew's charisma that they were ready to believe anything he said. Even Marcy found herself succumbing to his winning smile and invigorating personality. It was impossible not to be aware of the slight but consistent quickening of her heartbeat whenever they were together in the office hunched over a new form, a disputed order or the weekly sales figures.

If Marcy didn't know better, she'd have said Drew was nearsighted, because he always had to lean a little closer to read over her shoulder. She knew it was deliberate, of course, but she couldn't bring herself to move away from him and, frankly, she didn't want to. She enjoyed his closeness. The feel of his body pressing against her back as he hovered over her shoulder was warm and exciting and reminded her that it had been a long time since she'd been so vibrantly aware of the appeal of such a handsome man.

Yet she knew she'd have to distance herself if she expected to maintain complete control. It was Marcy's responsibility to keep the store operating at capacity, a feat that required her full attention. This was no time to get involved in a summer romance, especially with a fellow employee. Evidently Drew sensed her feelings and respected them. Though she was often aware of his eyes skimming the length of her body with obvious approval, he made no move to bowl her over with his masterful persuasion. This made it easier for Marcy to keep her responses to him in check. Still, she couldn't help feeling a little disappointed that his attention had diminished so drastically in the week they'd been working together. She knew she should feel relief, but she was only human. The nagging feeling of disappointment couldn't be stifled.

Marcy was posting a copy of the work schedule for the following month on the bulletin board in the break room when Drew came up wearing a look of total dejection. She could see, though, that it was more theatrical than actual.

"Is this Friday the thirteenth by any chance?" he asked.

"I'm afraid not. Why?"

"Well, to begin with, we're all out of apricot yogurt and that's the only flavor I like."

"How awful for you. . . ."

"Then I went over to the bakery for my daily cream puff, and they tell me they don't make cream puffs on Thursday."

"What a terrible disappointment that must have been." Marcy could feel a smile teasing her lips.

"On top of which, my car's in the repair shop. I was wondering if you could give me a ride home?"

"I suppose so. I'll be ready in about an hour."

"That's good. So will I."

It was after five when they left via the rear door. As Drew walked beside her Marcy had the vague feeling that he was crowding her a little, but it wasn't enough to mention, so she busied herself with digging her keys out of her purse. When they got to the car, Marcy discovered that another car had pulled in next to hers, so close to the driver's side that she'd never be able to get the door open. The passenger side had a little more room. Without a word, Drew took the keys out of her hand in one quick movement.

"Stay here. I'll back it out."

It was a statement, not a question, but Marcy didn't object. She hated dragging herself across the passenger seat and getting her legs and torso over the console. Drew backed the little compact out quickly and easily, turning it so that the passenger door was right in front of Marcy. Reaching over, he opened it, indicating that she should get in. She hesitated. It was one thing for him to back it out and another for him to do the driving. Marcy almost resented this transgression into her territory. She stood there, frowning in indecision.

"Hurry up," he said. "You're blocking traffic."

Marcy looked from right to left. There wasn't a car anywhere, but there were many customers in the side lot. She didn't want to create a scene, so she got in and slammed the door.

"I *do* know how to drive," she informed him. "In fact, I prefer it."

"I thought this would be easier since you don't know the way."

"I can follow directions."

"But I don't give them very well."

She slanted him a knowing glance but didn't answer. They stopped for a light, and Drew turned to face her. A smile ruffled the corners of his mouth as

his eyes roamed the soft curve of her lips. It was a
deliberately provocative gesture, intended to send her
pulses racing—it was successful. Marcy had the terrible urge to moisten the curve of her underlip with the
tip of her tongue. She wondered what his response
would be.

But the moment passed as he shifted gears and
drove forward. "As long as you have to put a label on
everything," he said, "why not write my actions off to
male ego?"

She nodded. "That sounds right, but don't you
think you're a little old for that?"

"Not at all. According to Freud, it gets worse as you
get older. I'm thirty-four now. I figure by the time I'm
ninety, I'll be impossible to live with."

"No comment," she said, but she couldn't contain
her smile of pleasure. There was no denying the mas-
culine force about him, the self-confidence born of
certainty and delivered with the frankness of the
practiced hunter. It sent her blood soaring, and she
found herself wanting to reach out and touch him.

Marcy shifted in her seat, embarrassed at her own
reactions. Fortunately the trip wasn't long. In fact, it
was only six blocks away, and Marcy wondered why he
hadn't just walked home. He pulled her car into a
parking space in front of a two-story apartment
house. It was an older building that had been con-
verted into four units, but it still had a charm, a
uniqueness about it that modern structures lacked.
The building surprised Marcy. She would have
thought Drew would go for the ultra-modern or a
singles place where the social activity was abundant
and close at hand.

He turned off the engine and pulled out the keys.
"How about coming up for a drink?" he asked.

"Oh, I don't think so. I have to be getting home."

"What for?" It was a challenging question, one she wasn't ready for.

"Well," she stalled, "I have laundry and other things to do . . ." Her voice trailed off, vaguely uncertain.

"I won't take no for an answer," he said as he opened the door and got out. "I've been cleaning all week just waiting for a visitor."

"I doubt that," she said, "but I suppose one drink would be all right."

Almost before the sentence was finished, Drew was around the car and helping her out. He put a firm hand on her elbow and didn't release it until they had gone around to the back of the building and started up the staircase. A soft breeze was blowing, and Marcy instinctively clapped her hand against her thigh to hold down her skirt. Drew was right behind her and she knew he was watching every movement. She could feel his eyes on her back almost as clearly as she could feel her own senses quivering with awareness.

The outside staircase led directly into a small screened-in porch overlooking the back yard and, beyond that, the canal. The voices of children playing could be heard in the distance.

"This is very nice"—she smiled approvingly—"but I'm a little awed at the wholesomeness of the atmosphere. It's not at all what I expected."

"Did you think I lived over a disco or something?"

"Frankly, yes."

"It just goes to show you how erroneous first impressions can be." He sighed as he pulled out two webbed lounge chairs and placed them opposite each other. "I'll bet you didn't even suspect I'd been living the life of a monk here."

"No, I didn't." She smiled with honeyed sweetness. "I'm still not convinced."

"Thanks." He grinned, playfully touching her chin with his fist. "Now that we've got that out of the way, how about a drink?"

"Fine. I'll have a beer with you."

"Beer it is. Come on, keep me company." Weaving his fingers with hers, Drew slid back the glass-paneled door that led into the apartment and pulled her into the cool interior, a surprising contrast to his warm grip.

As they crossed the dining end Marcy took in her surroundings with a practiced eye. Entering the small kitchenette, Drew released her hand to get the beers out of the refrigerator. Marcy stood in the doorway and made an obvious and thorough inspection of the premises. She made no effort to hide her dismay.

"My god." She shuddered as she did a three-hundred-and-sixty degree turn. "This looks like the inside of a garbage can."

Clothes, towels, newspapers, magazines and mail were piled everywhere. The largest stereo she'd ever seen took up most of the dining area, but it was almost completely hidden by stacks of records and cassettes. She turned back to the kitchen that was so full of dirty dishes she gasped.

"I thought you said you'd been cleaning all week."

"Well," he conceded with a slight shrug, "that may have been a bit of an overstatement. Actually, I have a cleaning woman who comes in twice a week and bails me out."

"From the looks of things, you'd better have her start coming in daily."

"Hmm. Who have we here?" He grinned. "Miss Prude?"

"No. Miss Organization."

He laughed, a big mellow laugh, and, throwing an arm around her shoulders, pulled her toward him slightly. Marcy could feel the featherlike touch of his breath on her cheek.

"If you really want to organize something, let's start in the bedroom."

"Not a chance."

"Living room? There's a large sofa . . ."

"No."

His mouth twisted in defeat. "The porch?" It was obviously a last resort and not too appealing.

"That will do fine." She nodded.

With an exasperated sigh, he handed her a can of cold beer and started edging her out of the kitchenette. Then he paused, his good manners taking over. "You wouldn't want a glass, would you?"

Marcy smiled. "Yes, as a matter of fact, I would."

Eyes blank with confusion, Drew looked around the kitchen, vaguely hoping a clean glass would suddenly materialize. "My cleaning woman's been sick for a week," he grumbled under his breath. "If she doesn't show up tomorrow, I'll have to buy another set of dishes . . . and glasses." He was suddenly struck with a new idea, and opening the freezer section of the refrigerator, he withdrew a frosted martini glass and held it out to her.

"Will this do?"

"Do I have a choice?"

"Not really."

"It'll do."

"Ah, you're a reasonable woman, Marcy Jamison." He handed her the glass and started out of the kitchen. Once again he put his hand on her shoulder, but this time he was behind her. The whole back of her body from shoulder to hip was electrified by his nearness. "So reasonable in fact, that I might even let you see the rest of my apartment."

Marcy couldn't help but laugh. "I'm sure it's a decorator's showcase, but the porch will do nicely, thank you." Easing out from under his arm, she led the way. With a resigned sigh, Drew followed.

The porch had originally been a large balcony, but someone had added a roof and screening and renamed it a porch. Though it was small, barely able to accommodate two lounge chairs when placed end to end, the view was pleasant and the breeze from the canal brought with it the scent of flowers. Marcy sat down and stretched out her legs. Carefully, she poured a few drops of beer into her frosted glass. The foam rose threateningly but stopped short of running over. She sighed with relief.

Drew had taken the other chair and was watching her maneuvers with profound interest. A smile of amusement ruffled his mouth as she urged a little more beer into the glass and set the can on the floor. Suddenly she lifted her eyes to his and raised her glass in a triumphant toast.

"To the Super S." She laughed.

"Why not?" He tipped his can in a responding salute and took a long drink. Marcy drained her glass in one swallow. His glance swept across her face with a glowing look of appreciation.

"You're a woman after my own heart," he said as he leaned back and crossed his ankles. "My ex-wife always wanted a mixed cocktail."

"Somehow I can't imagine you being able to handle all that."

"I couldn't. That's why I divorced her."

"Flimsiest excuse I've ever heard."

"Well," he conceded with a slow grin, "there *were* extenuating circumstances."

"I would hope so." Once again she became engrossed in the ritual of refilling her glass. "You probably ran around on her."

"Wrong."

"*She* ran around on you?" Marcy lifted a questioning brow.

Drew swung her the devilish look of someone who was enjoying a secret joke, and Marcy found herself waiting expectantly. It was an odd feeling, as though the very air around them was charged with the same excitement she felt spiraling through her.

Drew leaned forward, his elbows on the arms of the chair, his eyes on her face. "I didn't know you were interested."

"Of course I am," she answered quickly. "I'm a very curious person. Besides, having also been through it, the subject of divorce intrigues me."

"I see." He sat back. "Well, at least you're honest about it. The reason for our divorce was because her life centered around the golf course and the country-club scene and mine centers around boats and water. We tried to rationalize our different tastes by saying that each should be free to go his own way, but that just made the split wider. Finally, we just decided to call it quits."

"What did her father think about that? You worked for him, didn't you?"

His mouth flattened into a grimace. "Yeah, for twelve long years. His son and I went to college together and were both in the firm." He paused, thoughtfully. "But in all fairness to old Collins, I don't think he wanted to lose me and, frankly, I wasn't sure I wanted to give up my position in the firm. But"—he shrugged—"who was I kidding?"

She nodded in agreement. "I don't think it would have ever worked out. Even if you'd been able to tolerate each other, any opportunities that came up would have gone to someone else, you can be sure of that."

"Right," he said, taking another swallow of beer. "Besides, I was getting restless anyway."

"You wanted to go into business for yourself?"

He nodded. "I have two friends, also CPAs, who are fed up with their jobs. We've decided to join forces and set up our own office. They want to wait until the slack season is over and start in the fall."

"Will you be staying in Fort Lauderdale?" She hoped her voice didn't reveal the sudden tensing in her throat. The thought of Drew moving away had never occurred to her until this moment.

He nodded affirmatively. "Sure. We all have a certain following, old customers we've taken care of for years. That's going to be the basis of our operation for a while until we get established."

"I see." She nodded, relaxing measurably. And then she found herself wondering how many women were included in that list of faithful customers. Probably more than she wanted to know.

"Now," he said with a clap of his hands. "It's your turn."

"What is this?" she asked. "Show and tell?"

It was the wrong thing to say, Marcy could see that immediately. A roguish expression swept across his face but fortunately an inborn sense of propriety surfaced.

"It's *tell*," Drew assured her.

His voice was carefully sincere, but Marcy could see by the glint in his eyes and the slight quirking smile hovering at the corners of his mouth that he fully expected "show" to come later. Well, she smiled to herself, Mr. Bradford was in for a big disappointment.

She poured a little more beer into her martini glass and set the can on the floor, fully aware of his watchful eyes. "I'm afraid my marriage doesn't make a very exciting story. Roger was an electronic engineer with the Prentice Corporation. He was one of those people who was gung ho on self-improvement."

"Including yours?"

She nodded. "Especially mine. I had two years of college before I went to work for the Super S Corporation. I'd been working in the office there two years before I got married and my job advancement hadn't been too good. For some reason that galled Roger. He kept nagging me to improve myself; go to school, take night courses, get involved in company politics, attend sales demos and marketing seminars."

"I know what you mean. The list goes on and on."

"I tried to keep up," she admitted, "but my job was demanding and by the end of the day, all I wanted to do was sit and relax. Roger couldn't understand. He spent every evening reading job-orientated literature and expected me to do the same. He kept telling me if I wanted to advance, I'd have to better myself."

Drew shook his head. "Why didn't you just tell him to bug off?"

"Because," she explained, choosing her words carefully, "I didn't realize what he was doing. I honestly thought that he was right and that I was a born failure." She ran a hand through her tousled hair. "It wasn't until he changed jobs and moved to Dallas that I experienced a freedom I hadn't known in years. I felt like a kid on the last day of school."

"You didn't move with him?" he asked, surprised.

"No. The plan was that he'd go on ahead and line up an apartment and a job for me. That took three months." She shook her head. "By that time, I'd come to my senses and realized that Roger wasn't encouraging me, he was demeaning me. No matter what I did, it would never be right. In his eyes, I was a failure and always would be."

Drew tapped his fingers together pensively. "I don't see how he figured that. He probably just wanted someone to pick on."

"Well," she said, pouring the last of her beer into the glass, "he's got his chance now." Setting the can down again, she leaned back in her chair.

For several long moments, they shared a comfortable silence. Marcy was surprised at herself for confiding so readily in Drew. Normally she was reluctant to break open her past. She'd dealt with it at the time of her divorce and then sealed it in a tight container and buried it forever. She refused to let the ghosts of her marriage return to remind her of her shortcomings, though she knew they were unwarranted. Despite Roger's forebodings, Marcy hadn't only landed a position as a store manager, but she was doing a darn good job of it as well.

She glanced over at Drew. He was reclining with his head back, his eyes focused on an invisible spot on the ceiling. She wondered what he was thinking and took the moment to study his upturned face. But somehow her glance never got past his firm, sensual lips. She found herself wondering if his kisses would reflect the self-assertive, demanding side of his nature that she knew so well, or the masterfully persuasive, coaxing, side that she was beginning to associate with him. Or, she mused, snuggling deeper into her chair, maybe there was still another side to this fascinating man, one that he kept in reserve for intimate moments. She sighed. It was a delicious thought and full of promises for someone. But, Marcy thought wryly, not for her.

Drew nudged her foot with the sole of his shoe, suddenly snapping her concentration back to the present. He had a knowing grin on his face. She wondered how long he'd been studying her.

He swung his legs to the side of the lounger as if to get up. "How about another beer?"

"Oh, no," she said. "I feel as if I'd had nine martinis already. I have to leave, but I did enjoy it. I dread going back to my air-conditioned apartment after this wonderful breeze. I'll be glad when summer's over, and I can open the windows at night and get some fresh air."

"You sound like a fresh-air fiend."

"I guess I am. I spend every day I can at the beach. I love the water."

His brows lifted in an expression of pleasant surprise. "Then you're going to have to go boating with me someday. I have a little cabin cruiser I keep at Kelly's Marina. Do you scuba dive?"

She nodded, but a little hesitantly. "I'm not very good at it, but I do have my own equipment. I go out with that Captain Frank's Scuba School once in a while."

He nodded. "I've seen them out there, but they go too late in the day. From noon on, the water's too rough." He absently curved his hand around the toe of her shoe. "What do you say we go Monday? We'll leave early in the morning and spend the whole day."

"Monday?" she repeated.

"Yes. Memorial Day. We both have the day off, remember?"

Marcy clapped a hand to the side of her head. "Oh that's right. How could I forget one of my five yearly holidays? I must be losing my mind."

"You'll get it back once you get out there on the water." He squeezed her foot, hard. "It's a date?"

"Sure." She laughed as she tried to wiggle her foot out of his grasp. "That is, if I'm not on crutches by then."

"I doubt that," he said, moving his grip upward to

encircle her ankle. "Judging from the firmness of your legs, I'd say you have good strong underpinnings."

His hand slid higher, but before it reached her knee, Marcy jerked away. Drew's touch was as light as a summer breeze, but it sent a dizzying current racing through her. She knew he sensed her reaction, but if he was startled or discouraged, it certainly didn't show in his face. In fact, it seemed to have sharpened his interest. Could it be, she wondered, that he was one of those men who were always more interested in the challenge than the conquest?

Swinging her feet to the floor, she shot him a meaningful glance. "It's time for me to go," she announced firmly.

"What's the matter? Don't you like physical contact?"

She met his eyes boldly with the conviction of one who was in complete control. "Of course, but it depends on the circumstances."

As soon as she spoke she realized her voice had a certain daring quality to it. It was very subtle but evidently enough to stir the man sitting opposite her.

He stood up, his tall frame looming over her like a great friendly giant. Then he extended his hand to give her a lift out of the chair. Marcy could almost see the tremors in his fingertips and knew that the minute she touched them, the shudders would be transferred to her own hand, and then her arm, up to her shoulders . . .

"Come on," he prodded gently. "I'm not going to attack you, Marcy, I'm just going to help you out of the chair."

Quickly she put her hand in his, but that wasn't enough. He took both of her hands into both of his and, pulling her up, circled her arms around his torso. Suddenly Marcy felt her fingers tightening into the muscled contours of his back and was instantly conscious of two things: the warmth of his flesh and the tingling of every fiber in her body.

Drew held her loosely with one arm around her shoulders. Gently he smoothed a curl away from her forehead and then, bending his head, he kissed the tip of her nose.

"That wasn't so bad, was it?" he murmured, his eyes very close to hers.

Biting back a smile, she raised her gaze to the ceiling as though in deep thought. "Nooo," she murmured, slowly, analytically. "Not bad at all."

"Then why don't you try it?"

Her eyes blinked wide open. "Try what?"

"Kissing me on the nose."

"Why would I want to do that?"

"To share."

"Share?" she repeated as though she wasn't sure she understood.

He remained motionless, waiting, but she could feel his arm across her shoulders tighten. The movement was almost imperceptible and she doubted if Drew even knew she was aware of it. But the meaning was clear. He knew what he wanted and intended to get it. To her surprise, Marcy found herself intrigued, pleased and tempted.

Raising her head, she kissed him on the tip of his nose. Almost instantly she felt his hand curve into the nape of her neck as he pulled her closer, his breath warm and moist against her cheek. Marcy was vividly aware of his forceful virility as a potent dose of desire washed through her.

When his lips finally captured hers, she was surprised at the sensitivity of his kiss. It wasn't hard and demanding or cruel and ravishing, but gently exploring as though seeking an inner signal from her, an invitation for a deeper, more intimate involvement. She could feel the determination within him, but she realized Drew was letting her set the pace. Knowing this, Marcy found herself relaxing in his arms, savoring his kiss with a sensuous ease. Yet, at the same time her heart was beating so fast she could hardly move and an exciting shudder crept down her arm. Almost as though he felt it, too, Drew's hand followed the course of the tremor to her wrist, then skimmed back up again to cup her face in his palm.

She remained motionless beneath the pressure of his mouth, not wanting to encourage him, yet not wanting him to release her either. As the kiss deepened, however, and his lips moved over hers with sensually exploring ease, Marcy found herself responding with a hunger she hadn't felt in years.

She knew Drew was conscious of the intensity of her response, but he didn't press home his advantage. Instead, he pulled away slowly. His eyes lingered on her upturned face and Marcy stared up at him, her pulses still racing with pleasurable sensations.

Drew's mouth curved into a sudden grin. "Not bad for openers. Are you sure you don't want to see the rest of my apartment?"

"I'm sure." She nodded, struggling to get her emotions under control.

He wasn't easily discouraged. "Then why don't we go over and see your apartment?"

"Don't you ever give up?" She laughed, exasperated.

A wicked glint of amusement flashed in his eyes. "Not when I get so much encouragement . . ."

Marcy could feel an unwelcome flush of heat rising into her face. Must he read every thought she had? It was not only disconcerting but downright embarrassing. She handled the situation by pretending it didn't exist. Bending over, she scooped her handbag up off the floor and tucked it under her arm. When she faced him again, her expression was inscrutable.

"Thank you for the martinis," she said, extending her hand. "It was a very lovely party, but it's time for me to go."

Taking her hand he stepped back, allowing her a little more room. He even bowed slightly from the waist, the image of the perfect host. But Marcy knew the gentle throb of desire was still there, camouflaged somewhat behind his half-closed lids, but still alive and doing well. Oddly, she found this very comforting.

Drew accompanied her down the narrow staircase, but this time he decided not to follow but to descend by her side. With an arm around her waist, he wedged himself between her hips and the railing.

"I feel like a sardine," she complained.

"I'm only trying to be polite and walk you to your car. I don't want you getting mugged in my driveway."

"But it's still broad daylight."

He looked upward as though seeing the sky for the first time that day. "In that case, maybe you'd better stay a little longer. I can open up a gourmet dinner for us in two minutes. . . ."

"No." She smiled as they reached the bottom of the stairs and started toward the car. "I believe I'll forgo that experience, though I appreciate the invitation."

"It's always open. . . ."

"Thanks," she said dryly as she opened the car door and got in.

With a sigh of resignation, he closed the door and leaned his hands on the open window. "Are you sure you have to go?"

His voice and his eyes were so appealing that she felt like saying, "No, let's go back to the porch and take up where we left off," but that was just a fantasy. Marcy had more common sense than that.

"I'm afraid so," she answered, coolly polite. "I have a lot of things to do. And what about you? Don't you have anything to do?"

His mouth quirked into a seductively lopsided smile. "I don't really have much choice. For me, it's either a cold shower or a long walk."

# Chapter Five

As Marcy drove home from Drew's apartment, the laugh they'd shared as they parted still lingered in her heart and on her face. She couldn't stop smiling. For the life of her, she didn't know why she was so attracted to him. He possessed every trait she disliked in a man—impulsive, aggressive, impatient. But it was different this time, she told herself. Besides, if he hadn't been that way, she wouldn't have gone to his apartment and her dormant senses wouldn't have been reawakened on a rapturous wave of excitement. It was a heady feeling, one Marcy wished she could keep forever.

For the first time in almost a year, Marcy forgot to do her daily exercises. She found herself wandering dreamily around her apartment, trying to do little chores but not really being able to concentrate on anything except Monday.

Today was Saturday. That gave her just one day to gather her gear together. She felt a sense of panic that was totally unjustified. Her scuba gear was neatly stacked in a corner of her closet and ready for instant use. Her bathing suit, towel, and suntan lotion were wrapped and stored in her canvas beach bag. Why, then, the hurry? The answer was obvious. Spending a whole day with Drew, talking, laughing, lazing in the sun, made her head swirl with all kinds of romantic notions.

Marcy realized that she and Drew really didn't know each other very well. It was still only a surface relationship and much too soon for any romantic involvement. She hadn't forgotten the unpleasant sting of defeat that followed her divorce, and she wasn't ready to chance another rejection so soon. As much as she wanted to know Drew better, she understood the value of a cautious approach. Evidently he did, too.

Drew's action seemed to say that he'd go only as far as she permitted him to. Though she knew the power was there if he ever wanted to use it, she also knew he'd never force himself on her. This automatically put Marcy in control of any intimate situations that might arise between them . . . which was reassuring, but vaguely disturbing. Control brought responsibility, and she couldn't help but wonder if she'd be able to keep her emotions in check the next time he held her in his arms—or if she'd even want to.

Lifting her picnic hamper from a closet shelf, she started dusting it off, but her thoughts were miles away. Why would any woman give up a husband as exciting and attractive as Drew for a day of golf with her friends? Of course, Marcy realized that all divorces had deeper resentments than those that showed on the surface, but Drew's explanation had been too pat, too blithe—almost as though the whole marriage had never existed. It was very probable that he'd been hurt more deeply than he'd let on. Maybe he was just feigning indifference. She couldn't imagine him being coldly unconcerned about anyone; he was too passionate for that. Her body told her that much.

* * *

Marcy and Drew pulled into the store parking lot at the same time the following morning. His smile was broad and boyishly enthusiastic as he waved and strode toward her. As she watched him approach she realized she was beginning to find his effervescent personality almost irresistible. It brought a wide, warming smile to her lips. Then, suddenly, her eyes and her mind focused on his parked car.

She drew her brows together, puzzled. "I thought your car was being repaired."

He stood next to her, his thigh deliberately grazing her hip, and turned to look at his car, his expression as puzzled as hers. "Well," he drawled finally, "there really wasn't that much wrong with it." He flashed her a grin that was meant to be devastating. "As a matter of fact, I was able to fix it myself."

"I see . . ." She nodded sagely. "And what was wrong with it? Something simple, like Cindy's cash register?"

His face brightened when she gave him his answer. "As a matter of fact, yes."

"You're positively corrupt."

"But think of the rewards!"

"I'm trying to."

They stepped out of the way to let a car pass. Drew used the interruption to change the subject. "Well, we'd better get started," he said brightly. "What with the holiday tomorrow, I'll bet it's going to be one hell of a day."

"Probably."

"But don't overdo," he cautioned as they walked toward the store, "I don't want you wiped out before we ever get on the boat."

"I won't be," she assured him. "By the way, what time are we leaving?"

"Would six be too early?"

"Yes, it would."

"Hmmm . . . seven then?"

"How about eight-thirty?"

"Seven-thirty, and that's my final offer. We want to beat the crowd, you know."

"But I have to make the picnic lunch, you know," she countered.

"Oh?" His brows lifted approvingly. "That sounds great."

He reached out to open the door for her. As Marcy passed beneath his admiring gaze he turned his mouth downward in a clown-type frown. "Of course this means we'll be depriving ourselves of one of my gourmet treats."

Marcy threw her head back and laughed up at him. "And where were you going to get that? In the deli department?"

He gave her a slow, sensuous smile and leaned forward a little, his lips tantalizingly close to her cheek. "Don't underestimate my talents," he cautioned her in a low, deliberately suggestive voice.

Before Marcy could respond, they were interrupted by Larry, the night manager. He handed Marcy his checkoff list, eager to be on his way. She took it and started for the office and the beginning of a long, busy day. But her step and her spirits were as light as a summer breeze.

Marcy smiled when she saw Drew's car pulling up to her apartment the next morning a half hour early. It was a small apartment but had the advantage of being on the first floor, so Marcy had already put her heavy dive bag outside the door. As she closed the lid to the picnic hamper and dried her hands she involuntarily looked down to check her appearance. She was wearing a red broad-striped cotton shirt and white denim shorts with a narrow webbed belt. She also wore canvas shoes with nonslip tread, favorites with the local boaters. Her hair, minus much of its curl, was held back by a terry-cloth band.

Marcy opened the door just as Drew was hefting her dive bag into the back of his car. When he turned and saw her, his gaze traveled appreciatively over her scantily clad figure. He even let out a low whistle.

"God, you look great," he said. "I *knew* you were hiding something under that smock of yours."

Putting his hands on her arms, he bent his head and kissed her—a light kiss, a good-morning kiss. It implied the acceptance of each other as friends, and Marcy liked that. They were two pals who were going to spend a holiday together, no involvements, no complications, just a companionable, fun-filled day in the sun. Now, she sighed inwardly, all she had to do was remember that . . .

"Hmmm," he murmured, "you *smell* good, too." His glance swept the kitchen. "And so does the coffee. Where is it?"

Back to reality.

"Coffee I have, but I'm not cooking breakfast."

"How come?"

"I've just cleaned up the kitchen, that's how come. Besides, it's time to get going."

"But we're thirty minutes early," he protested.

"No, we're not." She smiled. "We're just getting a better start than we'd anticipated." She handed him the picnic basket. "But I do have a cup of coffee left in the pot. I'll pour it into a mug and you can take it with you." Hurriedly she took a mug off a hook and filled it with hot coffee. "Black?" she asked hopefully.

"No. Cream and sugar."

"You would."

Drew had a way of smiling without letting it show

on his face. At first, it had been disconcerting, but
now that Marcy had learned to deal with it, she found
it fascinating. She also found it fascinating to realize
that with very little persuasion, Drew would have hap-
pily spent the day in her apartment with her. In fact,
from the lazily seductive way he was looking at her, he
probably would have preferred it.

With the coffee in one hand, Marcy quickly scooped
her arm through the handles of her beach bag and
breezed past Drew into the warm morning air. "Don't
forget to close the door," she shot over her shoulder.

She could hear his sigh of exasperation, followed by
a louder-than-usual closing of the door and some
mutterings of discontent. It wasn't until they were in
the car that she handed him the mug of coffee. He
didn't take it from her, though, until she looked up at
him. His eyes were lighter than she'd ever seen them
and sparkling with a devilish glint, but she knew he
enjoyed their sparring as much as she did.

"Am I supposed to drink and drive?"

"That's right," she singsonged. Settling back into
her seat, she folded her hands in her lap.

As Drew took a swallow of coffee his eyes strayed to
the curve of her breasts, which were clearly outlined
by the snug-fitting top. He watched her for a moment.
Each time she inhaled, the broad red stripes widened
a little, then narrowed, then widened. Suddenly he
put the cup down on the console between them and
started the car.

"You're the meanest woman I know," he muttered
under his breath.

She nodded, agreeing. "Those are the chances you
take."

He grinned. "I see we have a morning philosopher
with us today, but does she know anything about

scuba diving? You must be certified or you wouldn't be going out on that Captain Frank's Tour."

"Oh, I am, but I've never gone deeper than thirty feet and I've never stayed down longer than thirty minutes."

"That's fine." He nodded. "We'll go out to the coral reefs. I just happen to know a spot that is, as yet, undiscovered by man. Except me, that is."

"Sounds exciting."

"It is. Full of color, too. The last time I went out I took my camera and was lucky enough to find a school of angelfish, or so I thought. But they went by so fast it looked like a parade of blue and yellow streamers. I didn't get a single picture."

Drew's animated recounting of former dives caught Marcy's total attention. His enthusiasm was almost boyish, and she found herself watching and listening with fascination. His vitality and his buoyancy completely captivated her, and she realized that something new was surfacing between them, something contagious and deliciously appealing.

Settling back with a languorous ease, she proceeded to study him freely. Her eyes traveled from his boldly handsome face down to his wide, powerful shoulders and arms to his long, tanned legs. He was wearing old sneakers and a pair of shorts that revealed the muscles of his thighs. They rippled when he moved . . . suddenly Marcy felt her throat close up. Averting her head, she took a quick, sharp breath to bring herself under control. That's just great, she scolded herself. All you need now is an increase in heartbeat, respiration, blood pressure and body temperature and you'll never make it off the boat.

Drew parked as close to the docks as he could get, but already the morning rush was on. Seafarers of all ages bustled around, loading their boats with food and supplies and making numerous trips from the parking lot to the docks.

Drew hopped out of the car almost before the engine died. Marcy had never seen him so excited. "Hurry up," he shouted over the top of the car, "I want to show you the *Sensation*."

"Okay," she said, looking around, "but don't you think we should take some of this—"

"No. We'll get that later." Her door was opened and Drew was pulling her out of the car before she could even uncross her legs. "Come on, she's at the end of this pier."

Drew's face was flushed with excitement, his eyes as sparkling as the sun on the water behind him. His whole body seemed to be electrically charged with an inner light that reached right out and pulled her into him.

With the slamming of the car door still ringing in her ears, Marcy found herself half running, half skipping to keep up with Drew as he pulled her along by her hand. The sun was high, the wind warm on her body. Marcy turned her face toward the salty smell of the sea and inhaled deeply. Her blond hair twisted out behind her. Reaching up, she pulled off the terrycloth band and let her hair swing freely in the wind as the marvelous feeling of being totally alive overtook her.

Suddenly, Drew pulled her to a stop. "There she is!"

He pointed proudly to the cabin cruiser berthed in slip number 54. The hull was a deep shade of mahogany, and the topsides and convertible top were a spotless and gleaming white. The seats and trim in the cockpit were Nordic blue. It looked long and sleek with strong clean lines, perfectly groomed and tremendously inviting. Very much like Drew.

He jumped into the cockpit and, turning, reached up to put both his hands around her waist and swing her down beside him. His face was positively glowing with pride. "Well? What do you think?"

"It's the most beautiful boat I've ever seen."

His smile widened even more. "Come on, I'll show you the cabin."

It was small, compact, efficient and absolutely immaculate.

"It looks like your cleaning woman has been working overtime," she marveled.

"Not on your life. When it comes to the *Sensation*, I do my own cleaning."

"It's fabulous. I've never seen anything so, so *sensational* in my life," she finished with a triumphant grin.

Drew flashed her a wide, devastating smile and, putting his arm around her shoulders, bent his head close to hers. She could feel his moist breath on her cheek. "You're a master of diplomacy, I'll say that."

"Just trying to please." She laughed, wishing she was as immune to his nearness as she pretended to be.

He must have sensed her inner excitement. "Ah, that's exactly what I was waiting to hear." Tucking his hand under her chin, he tipped her head back and kissed her, lightly, playfully. "That's your Welcome Aboard Kiss" he explained, his mouth inches from hers, "and then we have the Formal Initiation Kiss . . ."

Again his lips closed over hers. This time the kiss was more forceful, lingered longer, trembled ever so slightly. Marcy started to turn her head away but Drew, fully aware of her response, wasn't as eager to let her go as she'd anticipated. With his eyes still closed, he whispered into her lips. "And then there's the Marina Kiss . . ."

She felt his arms wrapping around her in a strong

and wondrously possessive embrace. Almost instinctively, she put her hands on his arms, then slid them up to his shoulders and around his neck, enjoying the way his muscled flesh felt under her fingertips. As his lips smothered hers boldly Marcy could feel the hot coals of passion begin to grow within her. With a quick intake of breath, she forced herself to avert her head, but Drew wasn't eager to let her go. Cupping a large hand at the nape of her neck, he held her cheek next to his. Their closeness was like a drug—heady, euphonic, drifting.

Drew lifted his head. "And then there's the Atlantic Ocean Kiss . . ."

Gently Marcy pushed him away. "Oh, no there isn't," she stated firmly. Then, putting her fingers to her lips, she blew him a kiss. "That's called the Weigh Anchor Kiss. It means it's time to get under way."

"Hmm. I didn't realize you were so nautical. I was sorta hoping you'd be a landlubber. Sometimes they don't even want to leave the dock."

"It's very seldom that you find a scuba diver who's also a landlubber."

Winding his hand into her tangled hair, he kissed her just below the ear. "Just wait until we get into open water," he teased her. His voice was low and purposely seductive. Then, turning around, he pretended to slap her on the derriere as, laughing, they both tumbled up the steps into the bright sunshine of a beautiful holiday morning.

It was almost nine o'clock when Drew eased the *Sensation* out of her slip and headed down the canal into the intercoastal waterway. Port Everglades was jammed with holiday boaters, and Drew turned his attention to the water while Marcy settled into the rear seat of the cockpit. She stretched her legs out so they'd get the full benefit of the sun and turned her eyes to

Drew, whose back was to her. He'd removed his shirt as well as his shoes and stood, tall and lean, swaying easily with the roll of the boat. The convertible top sheltered him from the blazing sun but, still, his hair shone like gold in the morning light. He reminded Marcy of a Viking, with his blond hair and sturdy legs and well-muscled body.

Drew turned to see what she was doing and motioned her forward. Marcy realized, then, that they were into the open water, passing the jetties and heading south. Putting her sunglasses on, she got up and stood next to Drew. He put his arm around her waist.

"As soon as we pass the Whistling Buoy, we'll head toward the coral reefs. We're in luck with the weather, I'll say that. I've never seen the ocean this calm."

"Nor this invigorating," Marcy added, inhaling deeply. "Mmm doesn't that salt air smell terrific?"

"If you don't watch it, it'll put you to sleep," he cautioned. "Better get some coffee. You did bring some, didn't you?"

"No. I thought you'd have some on board."

"I do," he confessed reluctantly, "but I don't want to mess up my galley. I've been up half the night getting everything shipshape."

Marcy stood back and looked at him with profound admiration. "Goodness, what have we here? Mr. Neat?"

An enigmatic smile curved the corners of his mouth. Gently he knuckled her cheek with his closed fist. "Just mess up my cabin and you'll see how fast Mr. Neat becomes Mr. Beat."

Marcy laughed. "But I *will* be able to use your precious cabin to change into my bathing suit, won't I?"

Turning, he cast a meaningful glance at the cockpit

as though studying the plausibility of using it as a dressing room. A smile of satisfaction touched his lips. "We'll see," was all he said.

Marcy gave him a playful pinch in the arm. "You bet we will." She laughed.

They'd been out about an hour when Drew "rediscovered" the reef he called his own and dropped anchor. With the engine cut, the sounds of the sea became more distinct. Marcy could hear the high-pitched wail of seagulls circling the boat looking for food and the water slapping against the sides of the *Sensation* as she rode at anchor, smoothly swinging and dipping with the rhythmic swell of the ocean.

It was so peaceful, Marcy simply collapsed onto the settee at the stern of the boat and idly watched Drew as he set the anchor and made his way aft, nimbly stepping down into the cockpit with a lithe, graceful ease.

Sitting down beside her, he clapped a hand on her knee. "How about a beer?"

"No, thank you, but I will have a cup of coffee."

"I see. Well, we do have instant. Do you mind drinking it cold?"

"Yes, I do. I want it hot—with cream and sugar," she added as an afterthought.

The grip on her knee tightened until Marcy yelped and swung away from him. As she turned, Drew circled her neck with his arms, pinning her against his broad chest.

Marcy laughed and strained away from him. "This is no time to fool around, Drew Bradford. We have diving to do."

He thought a moment. "Right," he said. Suddenly he got to his feet, pulling her with him. "And that means we change into our bathing suits." His face was as animated as his voice.

Marcy smiled demurely. "That means that I go down into the cabin and change into my suit while you sit here in the sun and wait your turn." She patted his cheek. "Like a gentleman."

Without waiting for his protest, she descended the stairs into the cabin, but Drew was right behind her. "I'll just get some towels," he murmured, crowding past her.

The area between the settee and the galley was so narrow that two people had to stand sideways to pass. Pressing her back against the butcher-block counter top, she tried to make room, but Drew never made it past her. Sliding his arms around her shoulders, he pulled her into him, gently cradling her face against his bare, suntanned chest. Marcy started to protest but a sudden, uncontrollable current of excitement spiraled through her. She could feel her skin prickling from the heat of his body. Even her breasts were tingling beneath the confines of her lacy bra.

His hand twined into her hair, and she could feel his breath, moist and warm, on her forehead. Pressing his lips to her temple, then trailing a line across her cheek to her eyes, he kissed first one long-lashed eyelid and then the other.

"Mmm, nice," he murmured, but Marcy couldn't respond. His body pressing into hers sent shocks of desire from the top of her head right down to the soles of her feet. Any plans of resistance she might have had were quickly forgotten as she slid her arms around his waist, enjoying the feel of his muscled flesh beneath her fingertips.

Their lips met in a burst of dizzying sensations. With her eyes closed, Marcy could almost feel her mind giving way and her body taking over. Slowly, Drew's mouth began to massage hers with a lazily sensuous movement and Marcy found her lips parting. Gently, languidly, his tongue entered her mouth and entwined with hers. Marcy felt a delicious heat shudder through her body as his arms brought her even closer. As she leaned into him she realized that she'd never felt quite like this before.

She was startled by the soft moan of pleasure that escaped her. With a shallow gasp, she turned her head to one side but still clung to him, her body swaying unsteadily with the roll of the boat. Reaching behind her, Drew grasped her shirt and pulled it out of the waistband. Sliding his hands upward, he unsnapped her bra.

"Let's get rid of this stuff," he whispered as he stepped back to pull her shirt over her head, and drop it to the floor.

His eyes fastened on her firm breasts, rising and falling sensuously with each breath she took. Reaching out, he cupped them in his hands and gently kneaded them, teasing the hardened nipples with his thumbs. Unwilling and unable to resist the aching torment of her body, Marcy closed her eyes and put her head back, succumbing to the stream of pleasure pounding through her.

Once again his hands were on her waist, but this time his fingers slid under her shorts. Without hesitation, she unfastened them and let them drop to her ankles. As she was stepping out of them Drew was easing her panties over her hips.

Marcy grabbed the band of his shorts. "What about these?"

"No problem." In one swift motion they were on the floor. Then, steadying each other, they pulled off their shoes.

Naked, they stood facing each other, their well-toned bodies shamelessly trembling with anticipation. Clasping their arms around each other, their bodies met in an uncontrollable burst of ecstasy. Drew buried his face in the curve of her neck and breathed hot, moist kisses into her skin. Marcy could feel a delicious rush of heat swelling from her loins to her throbbing breasts. As she moved to pull him closer she was suddenly aware of the almost imperceptible tremor in his hips and thighs. It was subtle and sensuous and more exciting than anything she'd ever known.

Cradling her in his arms, Drew kissed her again, a long, deep kiss that explored the inner recesses of her mouth with breathtaking sensuality. His tongue was as firm and tantalizing as his body, and Marcy could feel her knees crumbling as she was swept into a world of sweet bliss.

In one quick movement, he swung her up into his arms and, laying her down on the settee, he stretched out beside her. His body was as warm and damp as her own.

"Don't turn back now," he whispered with a tenderness that swept away all of her inhibitions, "please, Marcy."

She sighed contentedly. "I won't," she murmured as she reached up and, locking her arms around his neck, pulled him into the rising swell of her breasts.

His tongue voluptuously circled her hardened nipple, fanning the flames of arousal raging in both of them. Marcy moved her hands across his back and shoulders in a slow, rhythmic massage, reveling in the discovery of his firm muscles and the soft skin under her exploring touch. Her reticence long abandoned, she stroked his body with daring exploration, wanting to give this beautiful man in her arms as much pleasure as he was giving her.

She could feel his hand move to the small of her back as he rolled over her. Holding himself off with his arms, he pressed his legs against hers. They were as hot and pulsating as his body and sent a tormenting ache for fulfillment surging through her. A low moan of desire escaped her lips as she felt his weight bear down. Instinctively, her heated body arched against him as he entered her, and their bodies fused as one. Together they found their own wondrous rhythm and moved together toward the final and glorious unity they both sought.

As they lay clasped together they drifted down a gentle stream of pleasure into a smooth current of serenity. Marcy's spent body was still quivering as she snuggled closer to Drew and sighed contentedly. He caressed her neck and shoulders and then, lifting her head, he slid an arm beneath her and cozily fitted his strong body along hers. As Marcy's mind slipped into drowsiness a small smile touched the corners of her mouth. Where had she ever gotten the idea that she could keep her relationship with Drew on an impersonal basis? She'd known that was impossible from the very first day she met him.

Marcy was awakened by a slight movement beside her. Drew had pulled his arm out from beneath her shoulders and was stretching sleepily. He stopped when he saw that she was awake and planted a soft kiss on her upper arm.

"How you doing?" he asked drowsily.

Marcy nodded ever so slightly. "I feel like I've been drugged," she murmured.

Drew rolled onto his side and, putting a hand under his head, raised himself up on one elbow. His eyes scanned the length of their lean, tanned bodies. "That's because you're spent," he explained.

"I'm what?"

"Zapped."

"I'll go along with that." She nudged him playfully. "How about you?"

His mouth curved into a devilish smile. "Everything I have to give has not been taken, if that's what you mean."

Turning her head into the pillow, Marcy covered her eyes with her hand. "You're so diplomatic." She laughed, shaking her head.

"I just wanted to make sure I got my point across."

"You have," she assured him, "but it's time to get up. Besides, this cabin is as hot as an oven."

"I know. I've got all the hatches open, but the sun's terrific." Rolling over, he sat up and put his feet on the floor, but he reached back to put a broad hand on Marcy's stomach. "Maybe we'd better continue our exercises topside."

Gently she removed his hand. "Maybe we'd better get into our suits."

"Oh? So soon?"

She nodded firmly. "Besides, I should think you'd be starved by now. I know I am—for food," she added at the look he gave her. Swinging her legs beside his, she reached for a towel and wrapped it around her. As she was tucking the end in under her arm Marcy happened to look back at the settee, then shifted her eyes to Drew.

"No wonder there was so much room on this settee. You've got it pulled out into a bed." Her voice had a slightly incredulous note in it.

"That's because I slept on board last night. When I got up this morning, I decided I'd just leave it open. One never knows what one's going to encounter in the time span of one day." His hand closed over her knee.

She pushed it away with a gentle slap. "No one can ever accuse you of being unprepared, can they?"

"Not when I know you're coming on board." Kissing the tip of her nose, Drew stood up and pulled her with him.

Hugging the towel around her, she lifted her chin with a regal huff. "You, sir, are excused."

"The hell you say."

"Drew, we have got to get into our bathing suits."

"Then we'll do it together."

"Not a chance. You can change topside, and—"

"But the neighbors!"

"Surprise them."

He turned to go, then turned back again. Placing his hands on her arms, he kissed her firmly on the lips. Almost immediately, Marcy felt the renewal of very disturbing currents stirring within. Tightening her grip on the towel, she pulled away from him. "Drew," she protested.

"I'm going. I'm going." Sliding his hand to her hip, he patted it gently. "I just wanted to tell you what a nice package you have here."

"Yours isn't too bad, either."

It was the wrong thing to say. Instantly, his eyes flicked to the settee. "Then why don't we just . . ."

She didn't wait for him to finish. Turning him around, she headed him up the stairs. He went reluctantly, and grumbled under his breath all the way, but he went.

Marcy exhaled a long dreamy sigh and turned toward her beach bag to get her suit. How could she ever have thought of Drew as arrogant and pushy? He was the most compassionate, gentle, considerate man she'd ever met. He'd never take advantage of a situation just to satisfy his own sexual desires. She knew that if she'd offered any resistance at all, he'd have backed off. And Marcy liked that. She liked knowing that with him, making love would always be a mutual experience and that his pleasure would equal her own.

# Chapter Six

Marcy dressed quickly in her one-piece blue and yellow swimsuit. Picking up a towel, she ascended the stairs to the cockpit where Drew had stretched a blanket out on the deck. He was sitting on one end of it, the picnic basket opened before him. It was obvious that he'd been investigating its contents.

He watched her sit down and arrange herself on the edge of the blanket. As his eyes scanned her trim figure he gave her a low, appreciative whistle. Nodding, she flashed him a captivating smile of thanks, noting that he, too, was wearing a bathing suit. It was short and trim and gleaming white, setting off his broad sun-bronzed body to perfection.

Drew couldn't resist giving her an affectionate pat on the thigh. "Nice . . ."

"Yes. And it's also off limits."

His brows lifted quizzically. "For how long?"

The words "not very" were on the tip of Marcy's tongue, but she knew better than to encourage him. If he had his way, they'd spend the entire day in the bunk, and despite her constant awareness of his sensuous presence, she couldn't help but feel that things were going a little too fast for them. It was time to slow down, pause a moment to see where all this was going. She'd been swept into his arms and into his bed on a magnetic wave of passion, and she had no regrets. But

Marcy knew it couldn't go on forever without being rationalized. No man—not even Roger—had had such a strong and immediate effect on her, and she had to admit that she wasn't quite sure how to handle it. Despite her pulse-hammering reactions to Drew, she knew that a little caution at this point would go a long way to help avoid a possible disaster in the future.

"We'll see," was all she said. "But we haven't gotten any diving in yet to say nothing of lunch. I don't know about you," she said, pressing her hand against her stomach, "but I'm famished."

"So am I," he said, but Marcy thought she detected a lack of enthusiasm in his voice. This wasn't like Drew. He was usually hungry all the time. She watched as he opened the picnic hamper and brought out a loaf of bread. He laid it carefully on her leg. "What's that for?" he asked as he let his finger trail up her thigh to the edge of her suit.

She removed his hand gently but firmly. "Sandwiches," she said as she folded her legs under her. "I didn't make them up before we came because I thought the bread would get soggy. So I just brought the loaf and the ingredients." Her eyes twinkled up at him. "Don't you think that's a good idea?"

He paused a moment as if to let that sink in. "Yeah, sure," he murmured. Then, reaching into the basket, he brought up two jars; peanut butter and jelly. He held them out before him. "Now don't tell me, let me guess. These are the ingredients, right?"

"Mmmm." She nodded. "I was going to make chicken salad, but I was afraid it'd go sour in this heat, and I don't have an insulated hamper. But"—she laughed lightly, reaching into the basket for a knife—"nothing can go wrong with peanut butter and jelly. Right?"

"Yeah. Right. You can always count on peanut butter and jelly."

His disappointment was so obvious that she burst out laughing. "You're spoiled rotten, do you know that?"

His eyes roved over her with a boldly seductive glance. "Well, I must admit I'm used to the best."

The inviting tone of his voice sent shivers of delight through her. It was hard to pretend not to be affected, but she made a stab at it anyway.

"Just remember, you're the gourmet around here, not me," she cautioned. "Besides, if you don't like peanut butter and jelly, I brought some lettuce. Peanut butter and lettuce is always good. And then, of course," she went on, encouragingly, "there's always just plain jelly . . ."

"Or, just plain lettuce . . ."

"You've got the picture." Reaching into the basket, she brought out a bag of apples and set them down in front of Drew. "I was going to make some apple tarts this morning, but I was afraid they wouldn't cool in time to pack, so I just brought the apples. I knew you wouldn't mind."

"Of course not." He smiled bravely and peered into the basket. "And what do we have in that plastic-covered bowl? Leftover oatmeal?"

"It'd serve you right if it was," she quipped, setting the bowl down on the towel. "It's the lettuce, some celery, carrots, and cherry tomatoes."

"Cold?"

"Sure. I put them in cold water with some ice."

"Humph."

She scooped some vegetables onto his plate, then served herself and, settling back, started to spread jelly on her bread. Drew watched with such fascination that Marcy began to wonder if he'd ever been on a picnic before. Finally, as though he couldn't stand it another minute, he pointed to the tinned box in the bottom of the basket.

"What's in there?"

"Those are double-chocolate macaroon cookies. Homemade."

"Macaroon? You mean coconut?"

"Right."

"Double chocolate?"

"Mmmm." She nodded, biting into her sandwich.

Drew raised his eyes heavenward. "Thank you, God," he said, then turned his attention to spreading a thick layer of peanut butter on his bread.

Half an hour later, Drew was still sitting in the same spot, shaded from the sun by the convertible top stretched above him. He'd replaced the blanket with two mats and was sitting on one of them, resting his head back against Marcy's seat. She was sitting on her knees, leaning over the side of the boat and peering into the water, her body lazily relaxed and half asleep.

"It doesn't look very deep here," she commented. "I can see a school of parrot fish down there."

"It's about fifty feet."

"Oh," she said, slightly disappointed. "I thought we were going to go deeper."

His answer was a firm, "No. If we were going to do that we'd have to start real early in the morning."

"But at least then the water would have been cold," she protested. "Feel it. It must be eighty-five degrees."

Raising his arm up and over, he reached behind him and clasped his hand around her ankle. "It probably is, but it's going to feel like ice water on your skin if you don't get out of the sun. Besides, it's not a good idea to keep putting your fingers in the water. You never know what you might be attracting."

Marcy ruffled his hair playfully. "Then why don't we go down and find out?"

"Because we have to wait a bit until our lunch digests."

"Well, if you hadn't eaten so much, we wouldn't have to wait so long."

With a sudden movement, he reached back and caught her wrist in his hand. Then, half turning, he circled her waist with both arms and pulled her off the seat and onto the mat beside him. "I had to fill up on something," he said, nudging her in the ribs with his knuckle.

"That's some excuse." Marcy laughed. She was trying to make light of it, as if she wasn't aware of the aching in her limbs, but that wasn't easy to do when her body still throbbed with the memory of his tender lovemaking.

Raising himself up on one elbow, Drew looked down into her upturned face, studying her with a deliberately seductive gaze. His blue eyes were as intense as his taut muscled body. Marcy lay stretched beside him, so sensuously close that the web of arousal between them was almost tangible.

"Mmm, you feel wonderful," he said, laying a hand on her shoulder and massaging it lightly with his fingertips. Then he moved it down to the top of her swimsuit. Teasingly, he tugged at the straps, which she'd tied loosely in front when she was sunbathing. Grabbing at her suit, she tried to roll away from him, but he lowered his arm across her body, pinning her to the mat.

She started to protest. "Drew!" she sputtered, but even Marcy knew her voice lacked the ring of insistence that would have stilled his searching hands. Still, she strained away from him even though she realized that it was more as a duty to her former resolutions than a response to her present desires.

Drew's nearness was like a drug, filling her with a trembling surge of excitement. When his lips came coaxingly down on her own, Marcy involuntarily drew closer to him.

This time, his lips were strong, hard and more searching than before, triggering a new spiral of ecstasy that flamed along her body. Slowly, yet purposefully, she moved her hands across his chest and upward until her fingers were pressing into the strong tendons at the back of his neck. Moving her mouth with his, she devoured its softness, amazed at the magnitude of her own response.

Shifting his weight, Drew cradled her head in his arm. As his tongue moved hungrily over hers his hand skimmed possessively down her body and back up again to release her breasts from the confines of her bathing suit. Marcy felt as if she was dissolving under the tremor of his touch, and when his hands pulled the suit from her body and gathered her nude form into him, she was aware only of his eager trembling and her own swirl of aching pleasure. . . .


Marcy had no idea how much time had elasped, minutes or hours; she was conscious only of Drew's body beside her, completely relaxed and shamelessly exposed as was her own suntanned form. Marcy lay there in complete tranquillity, her mind and her muscles drifting in a sea of contentment. This time Drew had unleashed the strength she had sensed in him from the very beginning, but then, she thought, so had she. Together, they had shared one of the most intimate joys of living. Drew's lovemaking was an extension of her own desires, and the heights they reached were equal in intensity, a mutual revelation. Marcy knew that this wasn't, and never would be, a relationship where one partner demanded and the other conceded. Theirs was a shared happiness, and never once did Marcy experience the nagging guilt of her inadequacy as she had so often felt with Roger.

As her gaze scanned Drew's awesomely muscled body and honey-colored skin she could feel herself sinking into the rush of feeling only he could produce. She tried to think of a word, a phrase that could describe the feeling of total happiness that she felt at this moment. It was strange and powerful, something she'd never experienced before, something like . . . love?

Her eyes blinked wide open, startled. But as the word slowly penetrated her conscious mind, she realized it'd been hovering in the background for a long while. Marcy had been trying to will it away by hiding behind her job, her career, her divorce, carefully guarding her privacy by pulling into her shell. But that was over now, the decision was out of her hands. She was caught up in a whirl of sensations that she was powerless, and unwilling, to resist.

Did Drew, she wondered, feel the same way? She knew he had strong feelings toward her or he wouldn't have brought her out here in the first place, but was he ready for love? Or was he going to fight it awhile longer, as she had been doing?

With a deep sigh, Marcy rolled away from his side and sat up. Shaking her hair out behind her, she tried to comb through it with her fingers and was immediately aware of a nice, cooling breeze across the stern of the boat. Standing up, she let it waft gently across her hot damp body for several minutes before reaching for a towel. Licking her lips, she suddenly realized how parched her mouth and throat were. Noiselessly, she went downstairs to the cabin to get a drink of water and get into her swimsuit again. She noticed her gear was still at the foot of the steps. When she went back up, she took her dive bag with her.

Drew was up, stretching his arms and legs and yawning sleepily. He smiled when he saw her. "Good morning again."

Setting the dive bag on the deck, Marcy went over to him and, putting her arms around his neck, gave him a lusty good-morning kiss. His arms started to circle her waist, but she pushed him off with a gentle hand.

"Come on, get suited up," she urged.

His answer was a light squeeze on her arm. Then, wordlessly, he stepped into his swim trunks and went forward, put on his sunglasses and proceeded to stare vacantly out to sea. Marcy assumed he was still half asleep and needed a little more wake-up time or, perhaps, a moment of reflection? Were his thoughts scampering around with the same realizations as hers? It was an interesting thought. She wished she could see into his mind right now, but she knew better than to seek an explanation. She busied herself by opening her dive bag and laying out her mask, her flotation vest, fins . . .

"I hate to tell you this," Drew said, his voice deep with concern, "but we're not going to be able to do any diving today. The water's too rough and—"

"Too rough!" Marcy exclaimed. "How can you say such a thing? It's just as calm as it was this morning."

"It isn't," he stated firmly. "It's much rougher. You just don't realize it. Besides, I think you've had a little too much sun. You should take it easy and put some lotion on your nose."

"The little bit of sun I've gotten today won't make any difference on my skin. I'm used to being out."

Marcy realized she was sounding spoiled and pouty, but it was hard for her to give up something she'd looked forward to so much. "Why can't we just go down for fifteen minutes and find out?" Her voice had a pleading note in it.

"No. It's not worth the chance, Marcy. Remember, there's just the two of us out here. If something goes wrong, there's no one on deck to signal for help."

"People go diving in twos all the time. I've seen them."

"Not this late in the day. And don't forget, you're still a novice."

"You're being overly protective, Drew."

Closing the distance between them, he put his hands on either side of her face. "And why wouldn't I be?" Lightly he kissed the tip of her nose. "Next time, we'll get an early start."

She felt her defenses crumbling. He had the most charming way of refusing someone she'd ever known. "Well, whose fault is it we didn't get started earlier?"

He smiled with beautiful candor. "Yours. Though I confess I might have helped a little."

She drew her mouth into a sulky rosebud pout. "You brought me out here under false pretenses."

"Is that right? Funny, I was about to say the same thing."

"Chauvinism is dead." She sighed gustily. But she knew if she had it all to do over again, she wouldn't change a single minute of their day.

Drew took the "long way home," as he called it, giving Marcy a chance to see the shores of Ft. Lauderdale basking in the hot summer heat. The waterways were jammed with every conceivable description of watercraft ranging from exotic yachts to homemade contraptions. Despite the heat, the beaches were crowded with sun worshipers and bright-colored umbrellas.

Everything looked gay and festive, but for some reason, Marcy couldn't get caught up in the holiday spirit, and she realized it was because she'd gotten a little more sun than she'd thought.

She sat in the shaded seat beside Drew and watched as he maneuvered the *Sensation* away from oncoming boats, his eyes alert and searching. They spoke very little, but their silence was a companionable one. Marcy realized that people who loved the water as much as she and Drew did were content to just be on it or in it. Conversation was unnecessary when one was mesmerized by the throb of the engine, the pounding of the waves against the hull, the soft spray of salt water on your face when the boat turned into the wind.

It was late afternoon when they finally reentered Port Everglades and worked their way up the intercoastal to Kelly's Marina. Drew backed the boat into her berth, and then they both jumped out to secure her spring lines. Once that was done, the *Sensation* seemed to settle down in her slip with an almost human sigh of contentment. Drew patted her hull with the flat of his hand.

"She's glad to get back," he explained. Then, suddenly, he turned to Marcy. "How about you?" he asked.

"Oh, I'm glad to get back," she answered hastily, "but that doesn't mean I didn't have a good time."

"Sorry about the diving. I know you're disappointed."

"Don't apologize, Drew, I understand."

"Good," he said, giving her a pat on the bottom, "Now how about helping me get this cover out and secured over the cockpit? No previous experience necessary," he added hastily.

"I thought as much."

"But if you do a really good job, I'll buy you dinner."

"Sounds wonderful." She flipped back a lock of tangled hair. "But it better be at a drive-in, and we'd better eat in the car."

His eyes took in her rumpled clothes and then his own disheveled state. He nodded in agreement. "You have a point."

It was early in the evening when Marcy and Drew got back to her apartment and unloaded the car. Marcy brought in the picnic hamper and beach things, and Drew carried in her sixty-five pounds of scuba gear.

"Where do you keep this stuff?" he asked. "I'll put it away for you."

"In my bedroom closet on the right-hand side." She started fussing with the picnic things at the sink, but she was aware of the bumping and thumping in her closet as Drew tried to wedge her gear into the tiny space allotted. Finally, he came back to the kitchen.

"Boy, you sure have a lot of shoes."

"Mmm."

"And a double bed."

"Mmm."

"What do you need a double bed for?"

"I do a lot of entertaining."

"Mmm."

Marcy slid him an amused, questioning look. "I suppose you're going to tell me you have a twin bed?"

"I'd never say, but I *will* let you find out for yourself."

"I suspected as much." Marcy laughed.

Coming up behind her, Drew slid his arms around her waist and breathed a kiss into her hair. His body fit snugly with hers, and she found herself relaxing against him, enjoying the warmth of his touch, his closeness, the intimacy of a moment when their thoughts drifted together in drowsy warmth.

His fingers, as light as a summer breeze, trailed across her arm. "You know something?" he said. "I think you got a little sunburn."

"So do I." She nodded sleepily. "My skin feels hot and my eyes itch. Even the backs of my legs are starting to hurt."

"Do you want me to put some lotion on? Applying lotion happens to be one of my specialties."

"Well . . ." She paused. It was really time for him to go, but a few minutes more wouldn't hurt. "Maybe just on my back."

He was delighted to accommodate, and she sat in the chair with her back to him and held her hair up off her neck. As Drew's fingers moved rhythmically across her shoulders, she exhaled a long sigh.

His hand paused momentarily, then resumed its ministrations. "What's the matter?" he asked. "Aren't you feeling well?"

"I'm fine," she assured him. "I just have a nagging letdown feeling. Must be the sun."

"Sure that's all?"

"What else could it be? It's been a perfect day; good weather, a light breeze, a gorgeous boat and"—she looked back over her shoulder—"a very handsome man who is experienced in applying lotion."

"Then why the down feeling?" There was a concern in Drew's voice, and she was sorry she'd worried him.

"For some reason or other, I keep thinking of Roger. I haven't thought of him for months, but when I do, it's always connected with some goof-up I've made."

"Well, you didn't goof anything today, I'll vouch for that."

"Even a trifling error became a major crisis with him. I'm glad you're not like that."

He put the lotion bottle down and dried his hands. "For a minute there, I thought you were going to say I was." He edged his hip onto the table and faced her directly. "What's wrong, Marcy?"

She hated to admit the nagging feelings of doubt that were tugging at the edges of her mind, but she didn't want them to part with even a shadow of discontent between them. "I don't know much about the tides and swells of the Atlantic Ocean," she began, "but to me, the water seemed as calm when we came in this afternoon as when we left this morning."

"Oh, no," he argued, "there was all the difference in the world. Even at noontime it was rougher than when we started."

"I suppose you're right," she conceded, then lifted her eyes to his. "But was it rough enough to call off the dive?"

Drew looked at her, incredulous. "Is that what's wrong? You're ticked off because we didn't dive?"

She sat up, defensively. "No, that's not it at all. I've learned the importance of buddy diving in my lessons and I was wondering if—"

"Are you suggesting I didn't trust you?" Drew cut in. "Do you think that's why I decided against diving?"

Marcy blinked, a little stunned to hear her thoughts expressed so frankly.

She put her hand over Drew's and shook her head. "I'm sorry," she apologized. "It sounds so infantile, doesn't it? I didn't mean it that way."

"Is that what Roger would have thought?"

"Yes. He wouldn't have passed up a chance to point out my shortcomings."

Drew reached down and put his arm on her shoulder. "To me you don't have any shortcomings. And the next time we have a day off together, we're going to get started at the crack of dawn and explore those coral reefs until we're waterlogged."

Marcy smiled up at him. "That sounds wonderful."

"In the meantime"—he patted her thigh—"how about a little more lotion right here?"

Carefully she removed his hand. "I'm afraid not. I need a freshwater bath first so that I can soak the salt out of my pores."

"You mean to tell me you're going to take a bath after I've just put all that lotion on you?"

"Oh, hell. I forgot," she said.

"Don't worry. I'm in no hurry. I'll just wait until you get out of the tub, and I'll be right here to put it on again. In fact," he decided, as he stood up and started removing his shirt, "I might as well take a bath with you."

"Oh, no, you don't." She laughed, tugging his shirt down again.

"I don't take up much room in a tub. . . ."

"The day has come to an end," she reminded him.

"The hell you say."

But Marcy wasn't listening. Turning him around, she gently pushed Drew toward the door. He grumbled something about discrimination and social injustice, but he let her push him just the same. Until they got as far as the door.

He turned then, and they simultaneously reached for each other, their arms pulling them together. Swaying slightly in the dreamy silence, their lips met in a long, soft, lingering good-night kiss. It was hard to let go.

Drew's voice was a muffled whisper. "Are you sure you can manage that bath alone?"

"Sure," she whispered. He kissed her again, lightly, sensuously, and then, with a sigh of reluctance, he went out to his car. Marcy watched until he left the lot, then, with a final wave, she closed the door.

Turning out the lights, Marcy wandered into her bedroom and sat down on the edge of her bed. Kicking off her shoes, she got up and pulled her shirt over her head, then went into the bathroom, filled the tub and slid into the tepid water. She was glad that she'd confided her doubts to Drew. He was so compassionate and understanding, how could she ever have thought he'd have done anything but help her and encourage her so that they could enjoy diving together? If Drew said the water was too rough, then it was too rough. Who was she to argue a subject she knew nothing about? And who was Roger to insinuate himself into her wonderful day, creating doubts and uncertainties? He was her past, that's what he was, and he was going to stay there—forever.

Stepping out of the tub, Marcy reached for a towel and was immediately reminded of an earlier hour that day when she had done this exact same thing. That time, Drew had been stretched out beside her, his body bare and silky and shimmering with golden hairs. She'd run her hand lightly across his skin, enjoying the feel of it, the feel of him . . . she exhaled a long wistful sigh. Just thinking about Drew brought back the glorious sense of completeness she'd experienced when their bodies had yielded to the burning desires of their passion.

Marcy stared up at the ceiling, trying to tug her thoughts into focus, but it was impossible to concentrate. She could almost feel her mind start to blur as it often did when she was overtired or had had too much sun. Shaking herself sternly, she finished toweling and went about the business of getting ready for bed. As she dabbed the lotion on her sunburn she couldn't help but wish that Drew was there to help. Maybe next time, she thought dreamily. Still, her mind refused to focus. Funny how the sun and the heat and the water could drain your resources, she thought as she slid between the cool sheets and closed her eyes.

Without thinking, she ran her hand across the pillow next to her. Then, with a deep sigh, she closed her eyes and welcomed the oblivion of sleep where Roger faded out of existence and Drew lay down beside her.

# Chapter Seven

Before Marcy even opened her eyes the following morning, she was aware of the sting of sunburn on her shoulders. Rolling her head lazily to one side, she looked at the clock, amazed to see it was almost eight, a good hour later than her usual rising time. She'd have to skip her morning exercises if she planned on getting to work by nine, or earlier if possible. The day after a holiday was almost as hectic as the day before and every register would be open.

Swinging her feet to the floor, she sat up, vaguely aware of a nagging headache and a burning behind her eyes. She wrapped a terry-cloth sarong around her, fastened the velcro closing and made her way to the bathroom, where she plugged in her moisturized hair-roller kit. Then she went to the kitchen, put the coffee on and returned to the bathroom to inspect her sunburn—a lot for someone who already had a tan— went into the bedroom to get dressed, to the kitchen to pour the coffee, to the bathroom to set her hair, to the . . .

"Oh, hell," she said out loud. "I'm tired of this day already."

Leaning closer to the mirror, she inspected herself as if she was trying to see her headache, but all she could discern was the frown on her brow. She rubbed it with the heel of her hand and sighed heavily. She felt achy and irritable. She hadn't slept well, though she didn't know why because dreams of Drew had flitted through her head all night.

Marcy decided to skip breakfast, one of her favorite meals, and carrying her blazer under her arm, she stepped out into the hot summer day. As soon as she got into the car she put on her sunglasses, then turned on the radio. After pushing every selector knob, she couldn't find a program she liked, so she snapped it off. Then she started the engine, revved the motor and shot out of the lot. When she got to the end of the drive, however, she stopped and took a deep breath. She might as well admit it. This was *not* her day, but that didn't mean she had the right to inflict her rotten disposition on everyone at the store. She'd have to watch it today, avoid arguments and frustrating situations and remember to hold her tongue as well as her temper. After all, the day couldn't last forever. . . .

She parked next to Drew's car, glad that he'd gotten there early. The lot was already beginning to fill as shoppers hurried to replenish their cupboards. She went in through the back door and took aisle seven—canned fruits and vegetables, juices, spices and cooking oil—to the front of the store. To her amazement, Drew was bagging groceries. He waved when he saw her. She signaled back with a very casual wave. It was designed to throw off any suspicions the cashiers might have that her relationship with Drew was anything other than platonic.

As Marcy passed Louella's station she stopped and looked up. "Where are all the bag boys?" she asked.

"They're all here, but we only had three scheduled," Louella explained. "Who'd think we'd be mobbed like this at nine in the morning? Can you imagine what it's going to be like at the noon rush?"

"We'll be all right. I have one scheduled to come in

at ten and another at eleven." Marcy's eyes strayed to Drew, who was bagging and talking to an older woman who seemed to be delighted with the new "boy." "How's he doing with the bagging?" she asked.

Louella's face creased into a wide smile. "He's just doing great." She sighed wistfully. "The customers love him."

Marcy nodded, but she didn't trust herself to answer. She was afraid her voice would sound as dreamy as Louella's. Going into her office, she put on her jacket and was just sitting down when Thurmon, the manager of the meat department, came in. When he didn't take his hand off the doorknob and asked if he could close the door, Marcy knew it was trouble. She motioned him to a seat, but he preferred to stand.

"I no sooner got here this morning," he started, "when some customer come up to me with this package of rolled ham and says it's bad. I smelled it, and I'll tell you, it sure wasn't good."

"But he could have left it out of the refrigerator over the weekend," she argued.

"Naw, that's what I thought. I gave him a credit slip for a refund, but after he left, I opened up a couple other packages. They're all bad. Some are even tainted at the ends as if they'd been near some heat or something."

"Oh, good lord." Marcy sighed. "I hope no one gets sick. Did you pull them off the shelf?"

"Sure did. You want to see them?"

"Yes," she answered, getting to her feet. "If this is our fault, we'll have to take the loss, but if these tainted ham rolls are in all the stores, we can ship them back for credit." She followed Thurmon to the back of the store, hoping he'd kept the ham rolls under proper refrigeration. All she needed now was a couple more complaints and then someone would get the idea to sue for damages. She couldn't help but wonder if the cost of the lawsuit would be charged to the store. Probably, she decided ruefully.

All the ham rolls, which were individually wrapped, had been tossed into a box and placed in the cooler. Picking up one of them, Marcy handed it to Thurmon, who put it on the slicing table and cut it in half with a big cleaver. He handed it to Marcy, who smelled it carefully. She wrinkled her nose in distaste and put it down.

"Well," she said, thoughtfully, trying to assess the damages, "it's definitely not fresh, but it's really not all *that* bad. I don't think there's any chance of food poisoning here, but you never know."

"What do you want me to do? Send this stuff back to the warehouse or back to the meat packer?"

"I don't know. I'll have to call the main office and see what they want me to do. In the meantime, do we have anything else from this packing company in the meat counter?"

Thurmon nodded. "Yeah. Bacon, sausages and chitterlings."

"Why don't you do a spot check on everything?" she suggested. "It seems to me that this ham has been frozen, defrosted and frozen again. Could be the whole shipment's bad."

"Okay, if you say so."

Marcy nodded and, wiping her hands on a paper towel, started for the door. "I'll call Gail and get back to you as soon as I can."

"Right," Thurmon said as she swung through the door and into the store.

Marcy had taken a few steps when she was suddenly struck by the cold, ominous sensation that something was wrong. Stopping dead in her tracks, she looked around her. The store was empty. Half-filled grocery carts stood in the aisles, abandoned by their owners. There were no stock boys in sight, no shoppers, no kids running in the aisles, no babies crying, no voices or sounds of carts being wheeled down the aisles. The utter stillness crept icily into every nerve of her body. Suddenly, her eye caught the movement of someone running at the front of the store. Instantly she knew, with a chilling shudder of realization, that there had been an accident.

Making no effort to hide her fright, she ran to the front of the store. The cashiers were still at their stations, stretching their necks to see out into the parking lot, but the view was blocked by the crowd of people who had gathered in a circle.

"What happened?" she shouted up to Louella.

"Someone got hit by a car!"

"Oh, my god!" Dashing through the cashier's lane and out the front door, Marcy pushed her way through the crowd toward the red dome light that swiveled around and around with menacing authority. Just as she got there the attendants were closing the rear doors of the ambulance. She saw Drew talking to one of the drivers and ran up to them, her hand clasping her chest as if to still her racing heart.

"What happened?" she gasped.

Looking into Marcy's pale face and frightened eyes, Drew put his hands on her shoulders in a strong, reassuring grip. "Don't panic. It's all right. It was an elderly woman, but she's not hurt, just shaken up."

The driver nodded. "She'll be all right," he assured her. Then he got into the ambulance and it started to move slowly through the crowd as if there was no hurry, no hurry at all. But as soon as it reached the street the wail of the siren pierced the air and the ambulance moved forward with urgent speed.

Drew put his arm around her shoulder and lowered

his voice to a half whisper so that the curious onlookers couldn't hear. "Calm down. It's just a minor accident. That lady over there in the gray Chevy was backing out and bumped into another woman who was walking to her car."

"Didn't she look? Couldn't she see her?" Marcy asked frantically.

Drew dropped his voice even lower. "No, but I can't tell you why now."

"Wha—?"

"Marcy, I was out here. I saw it happen." There was an urgent tone to his voice. "Believe me, she wasn't hurt. It's okay." He lifted his eyes to the entrance of the parking lot. "I can't explain it to you now. Look."

Marcy turned to see a police cruiser pulling into the lot. When the crowd failed to make a path for him, he flashed his blue emergency lights and parked near the fence at the back of the lot before getting out. Drew started toward him. Marcy followed.

"Why don't you go back into the store?" he urged under his breath.

"No!" was her defiant answer.

"Then don't say anything, *please*."

Marcy's answer was a haughty "Humph." Who was he to tell her what to do in an emergency situation?

Drew introduced himself and Marcy to the patrolman, Officer Kaley. The crowd, opting to postpone their shopping until later, closed in around the patrol car, eager to listen, advise, and offer themselves as witnesses, whether they were or not. Leaning against the side of the cruiser, Officer Kaley listened patiently, taking notes on his clipboard. It didn't take him long to sum up the situation.

"The woman in the gray Chevy over there was backing out of her parking space and didn't see the woman behind her who had leaned over to pick something up off the ground. Is that correct?"

Drew nodded, but the bystanders didn't all agree.

"She wasn't picking up something. She was tying her shoelaces."

"No, George. She wasn't wearing shoes with laces."

"Then why was she stooped over?"

"How do I know? Maybe she had a kink in her back."

Kaley, long accustomed to the inaccuracy of witnesses, dutifully took down everything they said, but it was obvious he had other problems on his mind. "Who called the ambulance?" he asked gruffly.

"I did," Drew replied.

"Hmm. Why didn't you call us first? We're supposed to contact the ambulance, not you."

"I'm sorry," Drew said, his voice dangerously condescending. "I was of the opinion that health came before protocol."

Marcy felt her body tense. For the first time, she realized that under his calm exterior, Drew was furious. She couldn't understand why, but she knew this was no time for sharp retorts. Shouldering her way past Drew, she managed a small, apologetic smile. "I'm sorry, Officer, but we didn't realize that. We've never had an accident before and we were just so upset, we simply panicked."

She could hear Drew exhale a low disgusted breath, but he did manage to keep his mouth shut, Marcy noticed in relief. Officer Kaley nodded, satisfied that this would never happen again and started over to the car of the woman who had hit the pedestrian. Marcy recognized her as a regular customer and went over to her to see if she could be of any assistance, but the woman assured her she was all right. Her lawyer was on the way.

Marcy started back into the store. To anyone who didn't know her, she appeared as calm and efficient as always, but under that cool exterior, she was trembling with anger.

"I still don't have all the details of the accident"— she glowered at Drew who was right beside her—"but one thing stands out with glaring certainty. You took it upon yourself to handle the situation *your* way, with no regard whatsoever for company procedures, let alone *my* involvement. I should have been notified immediately," she went on. "It's my job, not yours, to notify the police and arrange for an ambulance. I would have handled it properly, along company lines, and the situation would have been dealt with speedily and competently. You overstepped the boundaries of your authority, Bradford, and what's worse," she seethed, "you knew it."

Marcy could see Drew was fighting to control his anger. "I have some unfinished business to attend to," he said, and without a backward glance, he started off toward the parking lot.

"And just where do you think you're going?" Marcy demanded, trying to keep her voice down so as not to attract attention. "I want to talk to you.."

There was no denying the steel in her voice, but Drew was not impressed. "I'm sure you do," he commented dryly, "but it'll have to wait."

With that, he stalked off across the lot, leaving Marcy as stunned as she was furious. Drew approached one of the stock boys who was leaning insolently against a parked car, hands in his pockets, ankles crossed. There was a surly expression on his face and Marcy recognized him as Ron, her least favorite stock boy who was always kicking through swinging doors and complaining about his job.

Marcy could see Drew mouthing a few terse words.

It was obvious his anger was at the boiling point. The boy snapped something back, and for a moment Marcy thought Drew was going to hit him. She couldn't imagine what was wrong but, again, it was her job, not Drew's, to handle any employee problems. With a long, determined step, she crossed the lot, but just as she got there, the conversation ended. Ron swung away from her, his face dark with resentment, and stalked across the lot to the back of the store.

"Well!" Marcy spewed, jamming her hands on her hips. "What was that all about, if I may be so bold?"

Drew's features hardened. "I just fired him."

"You *what*?" she shouted, incredulous. "What do you mean you fired him? Who do you think you are to—"

"Damn it, Marcy, will you shut up and get back into the office?"

Marcy stiffened as though she'd been struck. No one had ever told her to shut up. "What did you say?" she demanded, her voice low and smoldering with fury.

"You heard me." He was as furious as she was.

"I'm afraid I did," she retorted hotly. "You seem to be under the false impression that you're the manager here."

Drew's eyes swept the parking lot. "I believe you're creating a scene. Why don't we take this inside where it belongs?"

Marcy looked around quickly. A few people were casting them curious glances. "I don't see any crowd gathering."

"By the time we get through you will."

"Right," she retorted icily. Then, swiveling on her foot, she marched into the store, breezed past the surprised Louella and into her office. As Marcy closed the door behind her it took all the self-discipline she had not to slam it. She strode over to her desk, flopped into the chair and, crossing her arms, waited like an executioner would await his victim.

Drew came in almost immediately. He closed the door behind him—with a loud bang. He walked right up to her desk, placed two big hands on the desktop and leaned forward, his eyes flashing blue fire. Marcy could feel her skin bristling with anger. It was as if they'd suddenly declared war.

"Do you want to hear what happened or do you want to sit here and imagine it?" he snapped.

"I know what happened!" she shot back. "What I want to know is why I wasn't informed immediately. Why didn't you have Louella call me?"

"For one thing, keep Louella out of this," he blazed. "She had her hands full keeping the cashiers at their registers. Besides, she was busy calling the ambulance."

"And who told her to do that?"

"I did. In fact, I not only told her to, I ordered her to."

"You had no right to do that."

"Getting that woman out of the parking lot as soon as possible was vital."

"Why?" Marcy demanded. "You said yourself she wasn't hurt. If the police had been called first, they might have decided she didn't have to go to the hospital at all, and this whole thing would have blown over. Who are you to decide who needs medical aide, anyway? A brain surgeon or something?"

"All right," he snapped, "let's get a few facts straight—assuming, of course, that you're interested."

Leaning back, Marcy hooked her arm over the back of her chair in a dramatic display of patience.

Inhaling deeply, she met his eyes levelly. "I'm waiting with baited breath."

She could see Drew struggling to squelch a bruising retort. Oddly, she felt a twinge of guilt. She realized she'd been a terror all day long and was venting her frustrations on Drew. She watched as he drew a deep breath and, straightening, shifted his weight to his heels. His face was expressionless, as was his voice.

"Just before the accident, I noticed our good buddy, Ron, in the parking lot. He stooped down and did something on the pavement. I couldn't see what it was because of the row of parked cars between us, but I was suspicious."

"Why?" Marcy interrupted. "What was he doing out there anyway? He was supposed to be in the back."

"We were short of bag boys and he wasn't busy. He never is, unless someone's supervising him. Anyway, when I told him earlier that he'd have to bag and carry, he gave me his usual sour look."

Marcy made no comment. The stock boys knew they had to fill in as baggers when they were needed. It was part of the job.

"I'd just put some groceries into someone's car," Drew went on, "when I saw an elderly woman bent over like she was trying to pick up something from the ground. It was the exact same spot Ron had just left. Then, before I could do anything, I saw this car backing out of a space. I shouted to her to hold it, but she had the windows up and the air conditioning on. I tore over there and slapped my hand on the fender of her car as hard as I could. She stopped immediately, but it was too late. Her back bumper had nudged the elderly woman just enough to knock her over. I went to her and started helping her to her feet when I saw this."

Drew pulled a quarter out of his pocket and tossed

it onto Marcy's desk. One side of it had had a sticky substance on it, like chewing gum or clay.

"Our good friend, Ron," Drew said, "glues a quarter onto the pavement so that everyone would stop and pick it up. Of course, it'd stick and they wouldn't be able to grasp it."

Marcy nodded. "This trick happens about once a year in almost every store we have. Kids are always doing stuff like that."

"But not outside in the parking lot."

"That's true."

"And not maliciously. This kid was ticked off because he had to bag, and wanted to get even."

"Don't you think you're getting a little dramatic?"

"Not at all. In fact, I'm surprised you didn't get rid of him long ago."

"I had no cause to."

"Oh, yes, you did," he corrected. "The first day I was here, you asked him to do something, and I remember he answered with a surly remark and slammed his carton knife on the floor and stomped off. You should never have let him get away with that. He was insulting." Drew put his hands in his pockets and eyed her levelly. "No man would have put up with that kind of behavior for one minute."

Marcy bolted upright. "Oh! We're back to that, are we? Are you trying to tell me you don't think I'm qualified for this job?"

He sighed, resignedly. "Nothing of the sort, and you know it. I'm only offering a suggestion."

"Do you have any more?"

"As a matter of fact, I do." He perched on the edge of her desk as if he owned it. "No one knows about this quarter except Ron, you and me."

"And the woman who was hit," she added.

"She might not realize it was glued to the pavement,

and even if she did, she might be hesitant about mentioning it. Anyway, I don't think you should say anything to anyone. We could get into a lot of legal problems if some sharp lawyer decided we were negligent and caused the accident."

"But she wasn't hurt. What damages would there be?"

"A good lawyer will think of something, you can be sure of that."

"But it has to go into my report to the main office," she said. "Managers can't just make up their own rules as they go along. All accidents must be reported and every detail included. Of course, you wouldn't know about that," she added pointedly.

Marcy could see his jaw tense with renewed anger. "Then be sure to state in your report that when the police arrived, you took it upon yourself to intervene between an eyewitness and the officer making out the report. You don't know how much I appreciate your stepping in and treating me like a temperamental child."

"You were insulting."

"I was voicing an opinion."

"Keep your opinions to yourself, Drew, we don't need any more trouble."

"You seem to forget that *I* wasn't causing the trouble, *he* was. Whoever heard of a law that says you have to call the police first and the ambulance later?"

"It's not a law," she snapped, "and no one said it was. It's just routine. You might do well to find out about these things before you assume responsibilities that aren't yours in the first place."

He just stood there, bold and intimidating. "Is this a warning?"

Marcy blinked, confused and more than a little overwhelmed at the bitterness in his voice. "I don't know," she said, forcing all the self-confidence into her voice that she could muster. "I'll have to call the office and see."

She thought she saw a slight smile touch the corners of his mouth, but he covered it so quickly, she wasn't sure.

"I hate to sound efficient," he said, "but while you're doing that, why don't I go out and see if we're still in business?" Without waiting for her reply, he swung around and strode through the doorway. As Marcy watched his tall frame move out of sight, she was suddenly assailed by a terrible feeling of emptiness.

Putting her elbows on the desk, she dropped her head into her hands. What happened to her beautiful yesterday? she wondered sadly. How could she have allowed a petty argument over a company matter to come between her and the man she'd loved with such passion less than twenty-four hours ago?

In all fairness to Drew, she had to admit that he'd probably acted as anyone would have done under the circumstances. Her condemning censure of his actions was far greater than the situation demanded. What was the matter with her, anyway? Was she looking for a way out of her personal commitment to him? Was she sorry that yesterday had ever happened and trying to erase it from her life? No, she thought, with a firm shake of her head. She would never want that. Besides, it was imprinted on her mind forever—a day in her life she'd never forget.

Wearily shaking her head, Marcy opened a drawer and took out the accident report forms. Picking up her pen, she began to write, but the pen was dry. Irritably, she scratched it on a piece of scrap paper, but still it wouldn't write. She threw it in the wastebasket with such force that it hit the edge and bounced out again to roll across the floor. As Marcy leaned over and crawled a few paces to pick it up she was suddenly struck by the realization that the depth and seriousness of her intolerance bordered on the fanatical. You'd better get yourself under control, she growled to herself. And fast.

Her desk phone rang with jarring insistence, snapping her attention back to the present, to the job she had fought so hard to get and wanted so desperately to keep.

It was Gail. "How's it going down there this horrendous day-after-a-holiday?" she asked breezily. "If it's anything like the rest of our stores, you must be ready to resign by now."

"Close." Marcy's mouth twitched into a smile, the first of the day. It was good to talk to Gail and know she wasn't alone in her anxieties.

"Well, if you're beginning to feel as if you have all the problems, then listen to this," Gail went on. "We've got a whole shipment of brackish-tasting ham rolls out in the stores. If you have any, pull them right away."

"We already did," Marcy assured her. At least she'd done one thing right that day.

"Good. You're way ahead of us." Gail sounded proud of her, just the boost Marcy needed. "Now it's your turn. I can tell by your voice that something's wrong."

Marcy sighed. "We had an accident in the parking lot this morning. A pedestrian was hit by a car. She was taken to the hospital in an ambulance."

"Was she hurt badly?"

Marcy hated to admit she didn't know, hadn't seen the accident or the woman, but at least Gail would be a sympathetic listener. "I don't know," she confessed.

"My assistant manager handled the whole thing before I knew anything about it."

"Hmm." There was a thoughtful silence at the end of the phone. "Needless to say, this is frowned upon by our superiors." Gail thought for another moment. "Maybe it'd be best if you didn't mention this in your report. There's no line on that form that asks who decided to call the ambulance. It's just assumed the manager did if she was on the premises when it happened."

"Okay, if you say so, but there's something else," Marcy added, dreading the admission. "One of our stock boys glued a quarter to the pavement. It was when the woman stopped to pick it up that she got hit."

"Oh, hell!" Gail exhaled a long, exasperated sigh. "That's bad news. We could be liable."

"I'm sorry. I suppose I should have—"

"It's not your fault," Gail cut her off, "so don't take the blame for it. Besides, these things happen. That's why we have insurance. What about the stock boy?"

Marcy hesitated, not wanting to admit Drew, not she, had been the one to fire him.

"We fired him," she hedged.

"On the spot?"

"Yes." That was an understatement.

"Great. Shows you're acting in good faith. You've done all you can do, Marcy. It's out of your hands. Just fill out that report and send it into the legal department."

"I'm working on it right now."

"And cheer up."

Marcy couldn't help but smile. "Do I sound that bad?"

She could almost see Gail's gray head nodding. "That bad, honey. What's the matter down there? Is that ugly-looking assistant manager of yours giving you any trouble? Not that I don't think you could handle it. . . ."

"Oh, no. No," Marcy answered hastily. She didn't quite know how to answer a question like that, even to her friend. She'd have liked to confide in Gail, but she didn't dare, not on the office phone.

"Well, just don't let him push you around," Gail advised sagely. "Men have a tendency to take over—especially the good-looking ones, because they can usually get away with it. They're used to having women give them anything they want."

Marcy couldn't help but smile as she thought of Drew's aggressiveness. "You know?" she nodded into the phone. "You could be right, Gail. You just could be right."

"I know I am," came the firm response. "You just be careful there."

"Don't worry, I can handle Drew Bradford."

# Chapter Eight

In the days that followed, Drew and Marcy managed to keep out of each other's way as much as possible. When business matters threw them together, they were both careful to keep the conversation confined to problems concerning the store. Their exchange was always brief and formal and then, with polite nods, they'd go their separate ways. Neither discussed the argument they'd had or the angry words they'd flung at each other. By tacit consent, Drew concerned himself with the stockroom and employee relations while Marcy confined her activities to the office and the stacks of paperwork that never seemed to end.

Marcy had firmly decided to take the quick flash of anger that had erupted between them in stride, just because Drew lacked confidence in her ability to manage the store didn't mean everyone else did. She felt confident that she could handle any problem that arose and to hell with the doubting Rogers and Drews of the world. She was good at her job, and she knew it, and no one could take that away from her.

Still, the sting of hurt at Drew's condemning words lingered. They'd cut her deeper than she cared to admit. Perhaps that was because that was the last thing she'd expected of Drew. Somewhere along the line, she'd gotten the crazy idea that his feelings for her were as deep as hers had been toward him. How could he so easily dismiss that beautiful day they'd spent together and turn on her like a petulant child when he found out she wasn't a piece of fluff he could push around? Well, she could do a little dismissing herself, she decided. Who needed Drew Bradford, anyway?

Despite all of her rationale, Marcy found it impossible to get Drew out of her mind. One morning as she walked to the break room, she saw him at the far side of the store talking to one of the department managers. He was standing with his face turned away from her, giving her an opportunity to watch his tall athletic frame and his classically chiseled profile without his knowledge of it. Suddenly, an uncontrollable knot formed in her stomach, sending unwelcome waves of warmth across her skin. The day they'd spent together was still as vivid and as sensual as the memory of his burning kisses. Suddenly, Drew turned and faced her, catching her with his serene, compelling eyes. Marcy blinked and quickly turned away, terrified that she would succumb to the surging power of his presence across the store.

She hurried to the break room, cursing herself all the way. Had she paused to look at Drew because she knew that, ultimately, he'd be aware of her staring and look at her? If so, what did she want from him, anyway? she asked herself. Her trembling body was answer enough.

That afternoon, Marcy went about the business of computing their weekly break-even point, the number of customers per cashier, the average sale per man hour, the gross profit, the overhead . . .

Suddenly, Drew swung through the door, his eyes as blue as the sea, his body as bronzed as a Greek god. He went right over to her desk and, putting his hands flat on the top, leaned toward her as he'd done so many times before, she thought. The effect was like being blown about by a sudden turbulence of air.

Marcy kept her eyes averted, pretending to be busy with her work, but she could feel his penetrating gaze.

"Have you heard the latest news report?"

She looked up, startled. "No. What's wrong?"

"Hurricane Bonnie is on the way."

"Oh, no," she groaned dismally. "What else can happen?"

"I know how you feel." His voice held a surprising note of understanding. "But it's still far out in the Atlantic. It might swerve north and miss us altogether."

"God, I hope so. When's it supposed to hit?"

"If it comes straight at us, it'll be here tomorrow around noon. That gives us the rest of today and all of tomorrow morning to get ready."

"That's not much time," she murmured thoughtfully. "We'd have to put the shutters up, but I've no idea how long that takes. I wonder if the home office would know . . ." Her voice trailed off uncertainly.

"Why don't you ask Louella? She ought to know. She's been here for years, hasn't she?"

Marcy's face brightened. "Of course." She shoved her chair back and got up. She pushed her hair back and called Louella on the intercom, aware of Drew's eyes following her. She wondered if he could sense the quickening of her pulse—not that it made any difference. She could hide behind the hurricane.

Marcy motioned for Louella to take a seat. "Did you know there was a hurricane on the way?"

Louella shook her head. "No, but I'm not surprised. It's early in the season but it's happened before."

"It's supposed to hit tomorrow around noon unless it veers from its course," Drew stated.

"Don't worry. They're always late," Louella assured him.

"Do you know how long it takes to put the shutters up?" Marcy asked.

"You can do it in half an hour if you have enough help. It's getting the things out from behind the freeze unit that takes the time."

"I'll handle that," Drew said assertively. "Now, what else do we need to know?"

"Well, we have to get that outdoor carpeting in and all the carts, of course, but the worst of the storm is going to be the customers." Louella shook her head. "Everyone shops like there's no tomorrow."

Marcy nodded. "I remember now. I've heard other managers discuss it." She stood up, straightened her skirt and started to nervously pace around the office, her brow creased in thought. "They come in hordes, I understand, and practically clean out the store. We're going to need every extra pair of hands we can get."

"And open every register station," Louella prompted.

"You're right. I'll get two extra cashiers to fill in on breaks plus every bag boy and stock boy on the list." Her mind started to whirl with emergency plans and a backup system and a bail-out program and a—

"Are there any particular items they zoom in on?" she heard Drew asking Louella.

"Yes. Sterno, batteries, canned goods, water, soft drinks and masking tape."

"Masking tape?" he repeated.

"They use it on windows to keep the glass from shattering," she explained. "There's never enough of that."

"I wonder," Marcy said, more to herself than to the others, "if we could get a shipment in here tonight from the main warehouse?"

"It's worth a try." Drew responded.

"Right." Marcy sat down and started to pick up the phone. She looked at Drew. "Would you mind checking on those shutters?" With a nod, he turned to go. "Louella, take this list and see how many cashiers you can round up. Use the phone at your desk. . . . Hello Gail? Marcy. What are the chances of getting an emergency shipment in here tonight? We have a hurricane on the way . . . you can? Great." There was a long pause as Gail proceeded to tell Marcy what they'd need and how soon she could get it there. She sounded so efficient, it made Marcy proud to be part of the Super S chain. No matter what the emergency was, they always seemed to be ready for it.

By six o'clock the wind started to pick up, gradually but steadily, and by seven o'clock the store was so crowded that Marcy had to weave her way between the carts to get from the front of the store to the back. To her dismay, most of the shoppers moved with maddening slowness as each stopped to compare hurricane notes with the others. The general consensus of opinion was that the storm would suddenly change course and veer off to the north, hitting Jacksonville sometime late tomorrow afternoon. Marcy listened with half an ear, wishing it was so, but dreading that it wasn't.

They closed the doors at nine o'clock, but it was another half hour before the last customer left. Marcy was just starting to check the cashiers' drawers when Drew called to her from across the store.

"The supply truck just came in. I'm going to back to help Mort slot off."

She nodded, signaling that she understood. "I'll be back as soon as I'm through here. Then . . ." But her sentence was left unfinished as she turned her attention to the office register. The cashiers were, understandably, anxious to get home to attend to last-minute preparations of their own.

"If I don't get my lawn furniture in, it'll be all over the neighborhood."

"We have to take our aluminum awnings down tonight."

"My husband's sandbagging our patio."

"I'm taping every window in the house."

The preparations went on and on.

It was after ten before Marcy finally finished up and headed for the stockroom. Her steps were slower this time, as her adrenaline level began to ebb and the long day began to catch up with her. Pressing her fingers into the back of her neck, she swiveled her head slowly from side to side trying to ease her taut muscles. Then she took a deep breath, rolled her shoulders back and straightened her spine. From the looks of things, it was going to be a long night.

They had just finished unloading the supply truck when Marcy arrived. Drew, Mr. Morton, Larry and Kenneth were pricing the merchandise and loading it onto the uni-carts. They seemed to have everything under control and she felt a little guilty that she hadn't been there to help. When Drew saw her, he handed the freight bills to Kenneth and came over to her.

"Why don't you go home, Marcy? You look dead on your feet. We can handle everything here."

"But what about you?" she asked in a troubled voice. "You can't work around the clock."

"I won't." His hand touched her shoulder very lightly. "Thurmon is going to show me how to start the generator in case the refrigeration breaks down during the storm. Then I'm going home, too." His hands moved down her arms to her elbows, tightening slightly in a gesture of confidence. Its effect was an almost immediate wash of relief. Marcy knew that as long as Drew was there, everything that could be done *would* be done. And no one could expect more than that.

She regarded him with large, somber eyes. "I guess

you're right; I'd better go." She stepped away, but her body ached for his touch. "Maybe it'll blow over," she murmured, only half believing her own words.

He gave her arm an extra squeeze. "It's worth hoping for, anyway."

As Marcy drove through the crowded streets it started to rain. Hurrying into her apartment, she turned on the TV just in time to catch the emergency news release. Hurricane Bonnie hadn't changed its course and, at the latest reading, was headed straight for Ft. Lauderdale. The announcer's voice droned on and on, and Marcy snapped the TV off.

Sinking wearily into a chair, she eased off her shoes and, leaning back, rubbed her eyes. Her mind closed in on two things: the approaching hurricane and its disastrous consequences; and Drew's look of concern as his searching eyes looked into hers, reaching deep, with a quiet compassion that said more than words. She couldn't help but feel that the throb of desire that pulsed through her whenever they were together coursed through him as well.

But did they have a future together? They were physically attracted to each other, no question about that, but were they emotionally compatible? Suddenly, she shook herself, irritated that she'd allowed her doubts to surface so readily. It was a form of self-torture! Suddenly she pushed herself out of the chair and started to tape her own windows. It was time she faced reality.

Marcy finally got to bed at midnight, and then she only catnapped, not really sleeping but not wide-awake either. The sound of rain on her window brought her to full consciousness. It was only six o'clock, but her room was dark, and she instinctively knew that the hurricane they'd hoped would pass was heading their way. She dressed hurriedly, then

packed a small overnight bag with a few essentials to
tide her over for a day. Sometime during her sleepless
night, she'd decided to ride out the storm at the store.
She realized there was nothing she could do to prevent storm damage, but at least she'd be there to pro-
tect the store from its second biggest loss—looting.

Wrapping a rain cape around her, she pulled the
hood up and dashed for the car, literally throwing
herself into the front seat. The streets were almost
deserted, so she made record time and, within ten
minutes, she was turning the corner at the Super S.
Suddenly, she stopped, amazed. The lot was jammed
with cars, trucks, vans and RVs as people sat inside
their vehicles waiting for the store to open. Even the
spaces at the back of the lot were taken. Without hesitation, Marcy pulled up next to the building under a
huge NO PARKING sign and got out. To hell with the
rule book, this was an emergency.

Just as she stepped inside the door she was followed
by two of her cashiers, who came in breathless with
excitement. Louella entered soon after, then two bag
boys with Drew right behind them.

He came right up to her. "The storm won't hit until
around two o'clock," he said excitedly, "but I'm
getting those shutters up right away."

He hurried past her, motioning to Larry, who fell in
step behind him. It wasn't until they were out of sight
that Marcy realized Drew was wearing old jeans and
sneakers. Evidently he'd also thrown the rule book
out. Well, why not?

As Marcy hurried into the store, her ears picked up
the excited voices of her employees, who had all
arrived early as per Louella's instructions. Marcy
called them all together and thanked them for being
so prompt, then motioned toward the parking lot.

"Well, what do you say? Shall we open up?"

"Might as well," they chorused as the electric tempo of an emergency situation caught them in its grip. They all knew that the Super S *never* opened its doors before the stroke of eight.

The shoppers crowded in as if there was no tomorrow, but Marcy noticed that the almost carnival atmosphere of yesterday was gone.

"Everyone looks so worried," she commented to Louella.

"They know the hurricane's not going to turn north," came her grim reply, "and they're going to load their carts with everything they can get their hands on—just in case."

Marcy nodded, noting that there were no children in the store, just stern-faced adults who shopped with brisk efficiency.

Within thirty minutes, Drew and his hurricane crew had all the windows covered with the wooden storm shutters that were bolted into place with permanent fasteners. He came back in then and started helping the bag boys. Even Larry and Mr. Morton came up front to help carry out and Marcy and Louella opened the two remaining cash registers.

By ten o'clock there were only a few customers in the store. Though Marcy couldn't see the rain, she could hear the wind and knew it was time.

"Okay, it's time to wrap it up." She signaled to Louella.

With an acknowledging nod, Louella told the cashiers to close out their registers. As the last of the shoppers were hurried through everyone gave a sigh of relief. The cashiers immediately headed for the break room to get their purses and coats as well as their own bags of groceries. Their lively chatter echoed through the store as each expressed amazement at the rows and rows of empty shelves. The canned-goods section was a vacant hollow, the battery display rack stripped bare and the soft-drink area was devastated. The meat had been taken out of the display cases and stored in the main cooler. Only the few frozen foods that couldn't be jammed into the storage freezer were still in the cases.

Drew stood at the end of one aisle, hands on his hips, shaking his head in awe. Marcy came up beside him and together they simply stood there and stared.

"I've never seen anything like it in my life," he said.

"Neither have I. This is my first experience with hurricane mania." She shook her head. "I've never seen so much beer being checked out—"

"Oh, my god! They didn't take it all, did they?"

She couldn't help but smile. "I don't know, but I wouldn't be surprised."

With a groan, Drew took off disappearing behind the shelves. Then she heard a sign of relief, and he reappeared with two semi-filled cartons of imported German beer, the most expensive they sold.

"I'll have to make do with these." He grinned.

"It's fortunate you're so adaptable."

"You have to be in an emergency," he added grandly. He looked qustioningly at Marcy. "How about you? You want to take some of these?"

She shook her head but was pleased that he offered. At least he hadn't forgotten her completely.

Together they walked to the break room where everyone was scurrying to get their things together and go home. As they bid each other good-bye and wished each other luck, they ran to their cars, one by one.

As the last were leaving Drew turned to Marcy. "Why don't you go, too? I'll lock up." Without waiting for her answer, he reached for her rain cape and held it out for her. When she hesitated, he added. "This is yours, isn't it?"

"Yes," she said, "but I'm not going."

"You're not going yet?"

"I'm not going at all."

He blinked in astonishment. "You're not going at *all*?" he repeated. "You're staying here through the storm?"

"Right."

His surprise became edged with anger and disapproval. "For God's sake, why? What do you think you could do here alone? If the roof blows off, are you going to nail it back on again?"

"I realize my limitations," she retorted, "but at least when the storm's over, I'll be here to prevent looting."

"Looting?"

"Yes. I've heard that that almost always follows a hurricane."

Drew paused a moment to let this sink in, then eyed her slim figure speculatively. "I hope you have a black belt in karate."

"I'm hoping I won't need it."

"Since you only live a mile from the store," he argued, "why can't you just drive down here as soon as the storm's over?" Before she could answer, he added, "Forget I asked that."

They both knew that the streets would be impassable for hours, maybe even days, until the cleanup crews got out to remove fallen trees, wet leaves and other detritus of the storm.

As the last employee left Drew locked the door and slid the bolt in place. "Well"—he sighed expansively—"I guess it's just you, me and Hurricane Bonnie."

Marcy's eyes widened. "You're staying here?"

"But of course," he said, bowing elaborately from the waist. "You don't think for a moment that I'd abandon a damsel in distress, do you? Besides, I wouldn't miss the fun of fighting a gang of looters single-handedly for anything in the world."

Marcy laughed at his exaggeration. "I wasn't planning on hand-to-hand combat. I just thought if the store looked occupied, they'd leave it alone."

"And how were you going to make it look occupied? Stand in the window?"

"They're boarded up, remember? I'd have to stand in the door."

Drew had trouble controlling a smile. He let his eyes rake down the full length of her body. "And what will you be doing there? A bubble dance or something?"

"No! I just thought I'd walk around with a clipboard as though I was taking inventory or something until the store opened."

"You don't think the absence of cars in the lot would make them suspect that you were alone?"

"Hmm." Marcy hadn't thought of that. "Well, I'll come up with something."

"So will I," he said. He put an arm around her shoulder and together they walked into the store. "I'll say one thing, Marcy. You have more loyalty to your company than anyone I've ever known."

"Why wouldn't I?" She shrugged. "I like the Super S. They've been good to me. And despite all the problems we've had here, they've never once complained."

"They'd better not. Your work is faultless."

Stopping, she turned to him, her eyes filled with wonder at his staunch approval. "I'm surprised to hear you say that, Drew."

His gaze met her upturned face with quiet scrutiny. Marcy had the feeling he was trying to read her feelings and fit them into the overall picture he had of her.

"Why wouldn't I say that?" he asked, puzzled. "That's the way I feel."

She shifted her glance as though doing so would

curb the growing sense of awareness that she could feel building within her. Why was it that Drew's nearness always had such a shattering effect on her?

Shrugging indifferently, she managed to force a breezy tone into her voice. "I was under the impression that you felt you could handle situations better than I."

"What situations?" he demanded. "Are you talking about the parking-lot incident?"

"Well, yes, for starters." Suddenly the hurt she'd been nursing for days burst forth in a torrent of resentment. "Let's face it, Drew. The reason you handled the accident without consulting me was because you were afraid I'd louse it up somehow. Isn't that it?" Her dark eyes bore into his, demanding an answer.

Whatever reaction she'd expected, it wasn't his look of total bewilderment. Drew simply stared, obviously amazed at the accusation. As she watched him struggling to regain control the vague realization that she could be mistaken began to edge into Marcy's consciousness.

"I can hardly believe what I'm hearing!" His voice reflected his astonishment. "Do you really think I consider you some sort of dim-witted blonde?"

"Well, I—"

But he cut her short, and Marcy could see that his anger was on the rise. "I was only trying to get rid of a sticky situation as fast as possible. I was trying to help you, Marcy, not insult you! It never occurred to me that you were incapable. If you'd get your head out of the mud long enough to—"

"Mud! How dare you accuse me of—"

The lights flickered, the vast store darkened momentarily and then sprang into light again, an ominous warning that jolted them back to reality. For a

moment frozen in time they faced each other; Marcy
tried to mask her fear, but she knew Drew saw it in her
eyes. Without saying a word, he put his arms around
her and pulled her to him. His body was strong, solid,
secure, and all she could think of was, thank God he's
here.

His grip tightened slightly, then he released her. "Is
there anything you have to do before we're left in total
darkness?"

"Yes!" Her mind raced into gear again. "I want to
get the money in the pit and round up some candles
and matches."

"I know where there's a kerosene lamp. I'll try and
scour up some fuel for it." Turning her toward the
office, he gave her derriere a not-so-gentle tap. "Let's
move!"

Marcy ran to the office, but before she got there,
there were two sudden flashes of lightning and then
one terrific shot of thunder after them. Hurrying,
almost frantic, she started wrestling with the cash
trays, but it was hard to concentrate with the wind
pummeling against the wooden shutters. Her fingers
were stiff and unresponsive as she fumbled with the
coins. Several times she caught herself jotting down
wrong figures, miscounting the cash, forgetting the
coupon discounts. She dropped a roll of quarters on
the floor, and when she bent over to scoop them up,
she knocked a whole tray off the desk, spilling coins
and cash everywhere. Scraping it all into a money bag,
she tied it and threw it into the floor safe. She did the
same with the other trays. To hell with regulations—
she'd worry about them tomorrow.

Drew came in carrying a box and set it on her desk.
She saw a dusty kerosene lamp, some half-burned
candles and a bottle of pinkish liquid.

"We have several lamps back there, but the wicks

are a little short. I don't know how long they'll last."
He tapped the bottle. "But we do have a lot of rose-
scented lamp fuel."

"Hmm, no violet or orange blossom?"

"Sorry. You're going to have to go with the roses."

"I guess I can manage." She sighed. "How about
matches?"

"Cleaned out, but there are a dozen cigarette light-
ers left."

Another sudden violent whack of thunder held
them motionless. Marcy held her breath as the lights
shuddered for a breathtaking moment, trembled and
went out, plunging the room into total darkness. In
the windowless office, not even the faintest shaft of
light broke the black void.

"Quick," Marcy whispered urgently. "Light that
lamp."

"I have to fill it first."

"Well, hurry up!"

"I can't see," he complained.

"Light a candle!"

"We don't have any candle holders."

"Use a soda bottle!"

Drew heaved an exasperated sigh. "Now, how the
hell am I going to find a soda bottle when I can't even
find the cigarette lighter?"

"You lost it?" Her voice held a note of incredulity.

Suddenly, the click of a lighter brought a tiny flame
between them. Drew lit a candle and handed it to her.

"Hold it over here until I get this lamp started." He
wrenched the cap off the bottle of rose-scented fuel.

Marcy backed off a little. "I hope that stuff doesn't
explode or something."

"Believe me, so do I."

As Drew's blond head bent intently over the oil
lamp, Marcy concentrated on keeping the candle wax

from dripping on her fingers. They were so involved in their work that they barely noticed the violent screaming of the wind, the thunder, the torrential rain and the complete darkness of the office.

"There!" they exclaimed together as a rosy glow filled the room. They laughed, proud of their triumph over the failures of such modern conveniences as electricity.

"It's too bad we can't use this thing to cook with," Drew mused.

"I can't believe you're thinking of your stomach at a time like this."

"What do you mean? I've already planned our picnic."

"Picnic?"

"Of course. You didn't think I'd let us starve, do you?"

"Well, hardly . . ."

"You underestimate my survival instincts."

Smiling, Marcy looked up into the shifting lights of his eyes. "No," she said, slowly shaking her head, "I've never underestimated your survival instincts."

Putting an arm around her shoulder, Drew picked up the lamp and started out of the office. Marcy curved her arm around his waist, secure in the strength of his muscled body moving in unison with hers. As the fury of the storm ravaged the beaches, uprooted trees, destroyed power lines, flooded streets and homes and toppled utility poles, they strolled lazily through the store. The sturdy glow of their lamp enfolded them in a rosy aura of tranquillity.

"You know?" Drew said, looking around. "This place would make a terrific dance hall."

"Mmm." She nodded with a contented sigh. "I'll mention that in my next report."

# Chapter Nine

As Drew set the lamp down on one of the lunch tables in the break room Marcy wandered to the sink where a package of frozen fruit was thawing in a puddle of water. She held it up to him.

"Is this the lunch you've been planning?"

"Part of it. The best is yet to come." He opened the refrigerator, squinting to see inside.

Drew seemed so tall in his jeans and so handsome that Marcy found herself staring. Doubts as to her silent accusations against him began to tug at her conscience. His explanation of the parking-lot incident seemed so typical of Drew. He was an impulsive person who veered from the path of conventional behavior naturally. He was also a caring person. If he thought someone was hurt or needed aid, he wouldn't rest until he'd done everything he could for them. It was very possible that he'd acted in her best interest instead of . . . She paused. Instead of what? Just exactly what was she accusing him of? she asked herself. Of trying to make her look ridiculous? No, not that. Of treating her like an incompetent? Maybe something along those lines. Of acting like Roger? Oh God. No.

"There you go," Drew said, interrupting her thoughts. He gestured dramatically to the table. "Specialty of the house. Presweetened breakfast cereal with dehydrated apples."

"That's not too high on my list of treats."

"Ah, but that's not all. I managed to find a box of strawberries and several bananas." He put those on the table along with two cartons of blueberry yogurt.

Marcy eyed the assortment of food critically. "Are you some kind of a fruit nut?"

"No. If I were, we wouldn't be having milk on the cereal, we'd be having grape juice." He patted her on the head. "Now, how about a beer?"

"Oh, don't tempt me. I can't afford to relax in the middle of a hurricane."

He sat down and, leaning toward her, rested his chin against his closed fist, teasing, challenging. "What exactly *had* you planned on during the hurricane, Marcy?"

"I was going to stay in the office and guard the cash."

"I see. And what made you change your mind?"

"I've decided it doesn't need guarding."

He thought about that for a moment but couldn't seem to reach a conclusion. Finally he gave up and pushed a bottle of beer across the table. "Would you like to propose a toast? I believe it's your turn."

"All right." Raising her bottle she saluted him with a florid wave of her arm. "To the *Sensation!*" She laughed.

Drew paused and looked into her eyes, his brows raised questioningly. There was something special in his look, but then there had always been something special about Drew.

"I thought you'd forgotten," he said quietly.

Forgotten? The word echoed through Marcy like a shuddering sigh. Even now she was fighting the impulse to reach over and take his hand in hers and press his fingers against her lips. But, the haunting question in his eyes held her captive, infusing her whole body with the memory of tingling his touch created. Forgotten?

"I'll never forget, Drew," she whispered. "As long as I live I'll never forget that day." Then, huskily, she added, "But I thought *you* had."

He covered her hand with his, his touch gentle but firm. "I think about it all the time," he said. "I think about the sun and salty spray, the scent of your hair, the feel of your breath on my skin, the touch of your fingers moving across my shoulders . . ." Sliding his hand up her arm, he curved it behind the nape of her neck and pulled her toward him until their faces were inches apart. His eyes sparkled like star sapphires in the flickering light. "If you had the whole day to live over again," he asked quietly, "is there anything you'd like to change?"

He was still searching, she thought, reaching for an explanation for her sudden change in mood on that unforgettable day. But she couldn't bring herself to tell him her reasons; she knew now that they were childish and silly. She'd been a fool to compare Drew with Roger. The two men were nothing at all alike. Where Roger had always managed to make her feel inadequate, Drew was genuinely trying to help her. Why bring Roger into this now, she asked herself, and spoil this wondrous moment with Drew?

She shook her head firmly. "I wouldn't change a thing. Would you?"

He smiled. She could almost feel the relief wash over him. "I think next time we should go diving first. Then we'd have the whole day to get as sunburned as we want"—his eyes skimmed down to the V of her blouse—"*where* we want."

"What's the matter?" she said, looking down. "Do you object to the lines of my swimsuit?"

"Frankly, I object to the whole suit." He cupped a hand under the swell of her breasts, sending an astonishing surge of heat through her whole body. "I even object to this blouse."

"Are you suggesting I should take it off?"

"Either that, or I will."

"You certainly sound sure of yourself."

"I am." He ran a trail of kisses down her cheek but stopped at the corner of her mouth, leaving her throbbing with expectancy. "The minute I hung your rain cape back on the hook," he whispered against her skin, "I started waiting for this moment." He drew back a little. "How about you?"

"Well, I . . ." She stalled, hating to admit the thought had crossed her mind, and recrossed it, many times since.

"Never mind," he murmured. "I'll find out for myself."

His mouth was warm, very warm, on hers and moved over her lips, lightly tracing their delicate outline. Then, gently, he enfolded her mouth with his. It was a soft kiss, but it held a lingering headiness that tunneled under Marcy's skin and spread itself across her pulsing breasts. Lifting his head, he ran a thumb across her jawline. Then, without releasing her, he shoved his chair back and brought both of them to their feet.

"Let's get rid of this table," Drew said. "I work better alone."

"Me too," she whispered.

Stepping into his arms, she felt his burning hands on her waist. A tremor of desire quivered through her as she found herself being pressed into the corded strength of his body. Drew's lips claimed hers, tasted hers. Then, parting them with his tongue, he explored the inner recesses of her mouth, his tongue masterfully entwined with hers. A soft sigh escaped her lips as she leaned into him. She felt herself swaying a little, but Drew's arms were locked against her spine, firm, protective, yet almost unbearable in their tenderness.

Raising his mouth from hers, they parted for a moment. Even then, the sheer force of his physical magnetism made her feel as though she were still clasped to him. Skimming his hands down her shoulders, they moved to her breasts and roamed intimately over the soft curves in a sensuous circular pattern. Quivers of arousal trembled through her whole body, and continued to tease her. As soon as her nipples firmed his hand slid down the full length of her back and locked under the firm roundness of her buttocks.

"Hey," she said, making a pretense of moving away from him, "that's private property."

"I know, that's why I'm here." He gave her a provocative squeeze. "It's *my* property."

"Oh, no, it isn't," she admonished.

"We'll see." With a final pat, he moved his hand up her body and hooked his fingers into the waistband of her skirt. "How does this work?"

Laughing, she moved back a step, pulling at his belt buckle. "Same as yours."

"Shall we try it together?" he suggested as he pulled down her zipper.

Nodding, Marcy wiggled out of her skirt and kicked off her shoes. Quickly, she unfastened his buckle and unzipped his jeans, but pulling them down over his hips was a challenge in itself.

"Those things are so tight, it'd take three people to get you out of them."

"Think so? Watch my magic act."

In one movement, his pants were on the floor beside her skirt, and in one more movement, she found herself sitting beside him on the employees' cot.

"You move with great experience, I'll say that," she noted.

"That's nothing." He reached for the buttons on her blouse. "Wait until you see my next act. . . ."

Marcy laughed, taking his hands in hers. "Those buttons don't unbutton. They're fake."

"Then how do you get out of this thing?"

"It pulls over my head."

Together they removed the blouse and the rest of their clothing. The sudden exposure of her bare skin, the touch of his hands on her naked body, the radiant warmth of his eyes in the shadowy darkness brought with it an aching hunger. Rawly aware of the intense surge of excitement racing through her veins, she opened her arms and he came into them.

The sudden contact of their flesh sent renewed spirals of ecstasy racing through her. Slowly, expertly, Drew explored her thighs and hips searching for pleasure points, his touch light and painfully teasing. And then his hands slid over the swell of her hips, across her taut stomach, to her full breasts. Gently he kissed the hardened nipples, rousing a turbulence of passion that rivaled the storm outside. Marcy couldn't control her moan of pleasure.

Though his ardor matched the urgency of her own needs, Drew was not to be hurried. Taking her hand, he encouraged her to explore his body. Marcy caressed the strong tendons in his neck and lightly traced a sensuous path over his skin, across the firm lines of his back, his waist, his buttocks. A tormented groan escaped him and she could feel his chest heaving, but they took their time to explore, to stroke, to massage, to savor.

Drew sighed pleasurably. "You do good work. . . ."

Lifting her head, she met his eyes. They were brimming with tenderness and passion, beckoning and irresistible.

"So do you," she murmured. "So do you."

When his mouth came down on hers, she rose to meet him, her lips slightly parted, her body burning with desire. Suddenly she was aware of the subtle rhythm beginning to beat within her. Drew felt it and moving his body over hers, he closed his arms around her and encased them both in the flood of their own passion.

Marcy felt his weight bear down on her. Instinctively, she arched into him, her body reaching hungrily for the erotic pleasure only Drew could give her. They moved together in a surging rhythm of their own until, suddenly, their feverish bodies, taut with uncontrollable desire, climaxed together in a hard, fierce, final explosion.

Consumed, they clung together, letting the waves of fulfillment wash over them, blending their bodies into a final union. Breathing deeply, completely satisifed, Marcy was blind to everything but the sense of wholeness within her, calm and beautiful. Curling into Drew's arms, she snuggled next to him and rested contentedly. He was everything she'd ever wanted, she thought. Everything. Her love for him was deeper and more complicated than she'd ever dreamed it could be. It was hard to explain—like opening a door she'd never dared touch and finding a room full of roses. . . . Roses?

Startled, her eyes flew open as she awakened to the scent of roses and total darkness.

Drew's hand skimmed across her shoulders and

down her arm. "Something tells me we just ran out of lamp oil." He yawned, unperturbed.

"But it's so dark in here!"

"That's because we're in an inside room. No windows. The wind seems to have died down a little, though, so we're either in the eye of the hurricane or it's veered off course." He hugged her gently. "Frightened?"

"No." She shook her head. How could she be frightened when she was in his arms?

Raising himself up on one elbow, Drew gave her thigh an affectionate pat. "I hate to tell you, but I left the lamp oil and the candles in the office."

"Oh, no! How are you going to find your way through the store in this pitch black?"

"Hmm," he murmured thoughtfully, breathing kisses onto her cheek. "I'll tell you what. Since you know the store so much better than I do, we'll make a deal. You go to—"

"No way," she interrupted. "I don't make deals in bed."

"I was afraid of that," he said resignedly. Swinging his feet to the floor, Drew sat up on the edge of the bed. "In that case, we'll both go."

Stretching lazily, Marcy rolled onto her back and put her hands behind her head. "I was rather hoping to stay here while you went."

"Not a chance. I could get lost out there. Besides"—he squeezed her ankle—"I don't want to let go of you yet."

Smiling, she put her hand on his arm. "All right. I'm convinced. Let's go."

"You're a good woman." He started to get up, pulling her with him.

"Wait a minute," she protested. "We have to get dressed first."

"How can we get dressed if we can't find our clothes?"

"If we can't find our clothes, how can we find the office?" she countered.

"Ahh, I've figured that one out." With a final pat, Drew left her side and started groping his way through the dark. She heard him bump into a chair, then a table. Finally, a cry of success came from across the room as the tiny glow of a cigarette lighter flickered in the darkness. He held it up triumphantly. "Violà!"

Marcy blinked in disbelief. "Don't tell me you're counting on that thing to get us from here to the office!"

"You better believe it." He snapped the lighter out. "We can't waste it, though. Here." A soft swish of fabric landed on her lap. It was her skirt.

"Thank you," she said. "Where's the rest?"

"You don't need any more."

"Oh, yes, I do." She began groping around the bed. As she found her clothes she put them on, one by one. A movement beside her told her Drew was standing close, but before she could reach out to him, he bumped his shin into the bed. With a groan, he collapsed down beside her, his jeans grazing her leg.

He rubbed her knee with the flat of his palm. "I don't know why we're hurrying." His tone was vibrantly suggestive.

"I do," she said, gently removing his hand. "Someone might come in."

He exhaled an exasperated sigh. "*Who* for God's sake?"

"I don't know, but I'm not taking any chances." Her argument was full of holes, and Marcy knew it, but still, one could never be too sure. "All I need is my shoes."

Drew gave up. "All right." He sighed. "Let's look for our shoes. We'll get down on our knees and start crawling toward the table. When I saw 'now' I'll flick the lighter and you grab the shoes."

Marcy couldn't help but laugh at his organizational genius. "I think you'd make a marvelous field marshal," she said.

Even in the dark, she could feel his smile as he deliberately bumped into her. "I'd rather be doing this."

She could feel the warmth of his breath on her cheek and turned her face toward him. Their noses touched, then their brows, then their lips in a soft and comfortable kiss.

Marcy wished the hurricane would never end. Being alone with Drew, even in the darkness, was like a lazy day in the sun when her inhibitions blew away with the wind, leaving her completely free to let her passion soar with reckless abandon. The reward was the precious gift of ultimate satisfaction, so hard to find yet so much harder to keep.

"Operation Shoes" was not without success, though it took Marcy longer than Drew felt necessary. He kept hurrying her up. Finally, with their path just barely illuminated by the cigarette lighter, they inched their way to the office, trying to avoid such hazardous obstacles as abandoned carts and aisle display racks. Drew filled the oil lamp and together they went to the back of the store where he started the emergency generator for the meat freezer and the walk-in coolers. Instantly, the motors hummed into life, a reassuring sound to Marcy. She knew it wouldn't last out the entire storm, but even so it would buy them a little time.

As they walked out into the store Drew put his arm around her. "Let's think about food again. Somehow that lunch wasn't as satisfying as I'd expected—though I must say the entertainment was spectacular."

She punched him playfully in the ribs. "I hope you're not expecting a show after every meal."

"Why not?"

"Ugh!" She shook her head. "Men!"

His arm tightened around her. It was clear he hadn't given up hope.

Suddenly, as they neared the storeroom, they both stopped just outside the swinging doors and listened. There was a new sound, a whooshing noise that they hadn't heard before. They looked at each other, puzzled. "What's that?" they asked in unison.

Pushing open the door, Drew held the lamp up high. Water was bubbling in under the freight door and running across the floor.

"Oh, no!" Marcy cried out. "We'll be flooded!"

"We could sure use a few sandbags," Drew noted, but Marcy stopped him with a raised hand.

"How about kitty litter? We have plenty of that."

"Should work," he agreed. "Let's go." He handed her the lamp and grabbed a uni-cart. "Where is it?"

"Aisle six, center," she said, leading the way.

Quickly they loaded the cart and raced it back to the storeroom. As fast as Marcy tore open the bags Drew banked the litter against the door. Almost instantly, the water stopped coming in. Once that was under control, they fortified their dam with more litter. This time they didn't dump the litter out but slashed the bags to let the water seep in. Then, once the onslaught had slowed, they went back for another load. Finally, satisfied that they had conquered the flood, they set about the task of cleaning up the water on the floor before it ran into the stockroom and soaked into cartons of inventory. They worked steadily for two hours, and when they were finished, they viewed their work like proud parents . . . though their concerns ran in opposite directions.

Drew looked around him with proud amazement. "That's the best engineering job I've ever seen."

Marcy squinted and frowned. "I never realized how filthy this floor was."

Within hours, the wind changed from a shrieking howl to a "good blow" and, though the rain still persisted, it began to come straight down instead of pelting against the building on the horizontal. Drew and Marcy took several trips to the front of the store to peer out into the night. Once, far off in the distance, they saw the lights of a car wending its way through the deserted streets, a sure sign of recovery.

Marcy sighed with relief, "I guess the worst is over."

"I think you're right." He looked down into her eyes. "Sorry?"

"Yes and no," she said, meeting his steady eyes. Even now the ecstasy of his kisses still burned on her lips and the tingling sense of arousal only Drew could bring was throbbing softly within her, where she kept her most precious treasures.

"On the one hand, I'll be glad to get the store cleaned up and restocked. I hate everything hanging in limbo like this." She gestured around the deserted store, then squeezed his arm. "On the other hand, I can't think of a nicer way to wait out a hurricane."

"Neither can I." Even in the dark, she could feel the magnetism of his smile. "And the best part is, it isn't over until the electricity comes back on."

"That could be days . . ."

"What a shame." Leaning over, Drew kissed the top of her head and put his arm around her.

Together they wandered down the aisles by lamplight, leisurely selecting ingredients for their evening meal, laughing, joking, taking their time, enjoying each other.

Marcy, still drowsy from a wonderful night of lovemaking and contentment, walked with Drew to the front of the store. As she watched his hand gripping the base of the lamp she realized that this was likely the last time they'd make this trip by the glow of an amber light. It made her feel reluctant to start the new day, as though she was grappling with the dawn for possession of the night.

Nothing could change the intimacy of the hours they'd spent together, loving, caring and touching as each satiated the desires of the other. But Marcy couldn't help wondering if she really knew Drew any better now than she did yesterday at this time. Of course, she knew every muscle of his body, every movement of his lips, but beyond that, she had the feeling that he was reluctant to confide his innermost secrets to her. She was a bit worried. Didn't he trust her? Was there a question between them that was unasked, and unanswerable?

Drew pinched her playfully, bringing her out of her reverie. She smiled up at him and was rewarded by his sudden irresistible smile, the kind that washed away the raindrops and hustled forth the sun. Why was she always so apprehensive? she wondered as she bumped against Drew's hip. For heaven's sake, what more could she ask for?

Drew propped open the front door and stepped out into the muggy dawn. Marcy followed, a little skittish about leaving the security of the Super S, but a warm air current brought the promise of the sunrise, despite the storm. A few cars were moving cautiously through the debris, the utility trucks were out and people were beginning to move around, surveying the damage. Sheets of aluminum siding, twisted signs and strips of roofing mixed with loose fronds and uprooted fauna and rubbish. As Marcy walked around the building she was relieved to see that the Super S had come through the storm unscathed by wind or rain, but as they came back to the front of the building she spied a grocery cart smashed against a light pole.

"Look at that." She pointed. "Those were all supposed to have been brought inside."

"Well, you have to admit we were in a hurry," Drew reasoned. "Be grateful that's the only one out."

"Yeah, I suppose," she said, but she found it hard to relinquish even that one cart. Her dissatisfaction must have shown on her face.

"Come on," Drew teased, "don't tell me you're going to let that one cart throw you."

"No, of course not. But they do cost seventy dollars apiece."

"If that's all the Super S lost, they should be delirious with joy." He slanted her a glance, nodding. "And they have you to thank for it. If you hadn't decided to stay, they'd have had a nice flood in the stockroom."

"But you helped—"

"That's not the point," he said. "If you hadn't stayed, you can bet your last dollar I wouldn't have either." He caught her hand and pulled her along. "Come on, let's go talk to these guys on the utility truck and see how long it's going to be before we have power."

Marcy twisted her head to look back at the store. "But what about looters?"

"Oh, my God, you worry about everything!" Tightening his grip, he tucked her arm under his and hustled her out of the lot.

The supervisor of the maintenance crew assured

them they'd have power before the end of the day.
"We were lucky this time," he said. "We have a lot of
lines down, but very few poles went over."

"How does the marina look?" Drew asked.

"Not bad at all. We didn't have any tidal waves, you
know. A few boats got loose, I guess, and that's about
all."

"Good." Drew nodded.

Marcy felt a little guilty. She'd forgotten all about
the *Sensation* in her concern for the store. She realized
it must have been on Drew's mind all through the hurricane, though he never mentioned it. She felt a little
disappointed that he hadn't confided in her. Did he
think she was so involved with her own problems that
she didn't care about his?

As they were walking back to the store she asked
him about it. "You know, I forgot all about the *Sensation*," she began.

"As a matter of fact . . ." He smiled, deliberately
bumping against her hip. "So did I."

She couldn't help but smile to herself. So much for
her personal analyses. Maybe she'd better stick to
management. She seemed to do better there.

Drew volunteered to stay at the store while Marcy
went home to bathe and change. Mr. Morton arrived
just as she was leaving and volunteered to help Drew
remove the shutters. Satisfied that recovery was
under way, Marcy drove home through the cluttered
streets, marveling at her twofold stroke of luck. Not
only had the Super S suffered minimal damage, but
she had just spent the most beautiful twenty-four
hours she could remember. A soft smile touched her
lips as she recalled their hours together and the amazing sense of completeness they both felt—physically,
mentally and emotionally. As the fragments of her life
began to come together Marcy knew the focal point of

this new awakening was Drew. For the first time since she'd known him, she allowed herself to think of spending the rest of her life with him. It was a heady thought, filled with all sorts of pleasures, exciting dreams that made the gray morning look like a rosy sunrise.

Mop-up operations were under way by the time Marcy returned to the store. The shutters were down, the parking lot had been swept and the freight door was propped open. Drew and Mr. Morton had just finished cleaning up the kitty litter and were leaning on their brooms watching her approach. Drew had stripped to the waist, and his muscular body was still damp with perspiration. He looked so deliciously appealing that Marcy had to fight the urge to run up and throw her arms around him. She realized this was no time for romantic notions, but it was hard to ignore the erratic rhythm of her heart. She wondered if he felt it, too.

Suddenly, just as she reached out to touch Drew, the electricity came back on, and the store burst into a flood of light. Simultaneously, they all yelled "Hurrah," then stood at the freight door, staring into the store as though they'd never seen it before. Drew gave Marcy's arm a reassuring squeeze.

"We made it!" He smiled, his enthusiasm almost as great as hers.

Without another word, they all went into the store. Drew looked for leaks in the roof, Mr. Morton inspected the devastated canned-food shelves and Marcy headed for the freezers to see how the frozen foods had fared. As near as she could tell, everything was in good shape.

"We were sure lucky," she said to Drew moments later. "I don't think we lost a single pea pod. Of course we'll still have to have a hurricane damage sale, but at least Glen can pick and choose what he wants to get rid of."

Drew looked puzzled. "I don't understand."

"It's simple," she explained. "After a hurricane everyone expects a sale on what thawed during the blackout. If you don't have one, they think you just refroze everything and they won't buy it."

"Did it ever occur to them we might have a standby generator?"

"Evidently not." She laughed. "But at least we can get rid of those waxed beans and the prunes and the lemon cakes." She rubbed her chin thoughtfully. "Maybe I should call Gail and see if we can get some more frozen pizzas in here. They'd sell like crazy, don't you think?"

Exhaling a long sigh, Drew threw his arm around her shoulder. "Don't ask me such difficult questions. I haven't gotten past the waxed beans yet."

"That's because your mind and your body are both exhausted. Why don't you go home and catch a nap? I'll stick around here for a while and call the home office."

"But I'll see you later, won't I?"

"Of course." Already Marcy was wishing the day was over. "Let's make it my house for dinner."

She could feel his breath in her hair, blatantly seductive.

"That sounds more like it." He eyes sparkled wickedly. "Around three o'clock then?"

She was pleased at his attempt to hustle her, but she refused to be hurried. "Make that seven."

"Seven!" Drew groaned. "What in the world are you going to do between now and seven?"

"I'm going to get dinner, among other things."

Gently she turned him toward the door and gave him a friendly push. "Don't be late."

"Don't worry," he assured her with an affectionate smile.

Marcy felt a deep warmth flow through her as she watched him leave. It was hard to bring her attention back to minding the store when her whole body ached to be with Drew. She consoled herself with visions of a beautiful dinner, candlelight, just the two of them together . . .

With a firm shake of her head, she walked to the office and dialed her supervisor. When Gail's voice came over the line it was light and enthusiastic, which was surprising. Marcy had expected her to be concerned about the amount of damage done by the hurricane.

Marcy explained the loss of the grocery cart and the thirty or so bags of kitty litter they'd used. She didn't elaborate on Drew spending the night with her, though she knew Gail probably suspected as much. But if she didn't feel it should go into the report, why should Marcy make an issue of it?

"Well, I'll say one thing, Marcy," Gail raved, "you've done a marvelous job with that store. Your net profit is higher than any store we have, and believe me, honey, it hasn't gone unnoticed around here." Her voice dropped to a conspiratorial whisper. "Everyone's talking about it."

"What do you mean?" Marcy asked. "What's there to talk about?"

"Well," Gail began, and Marcy could tell by the hollow sound of her voice that she had her hand up to her mouth to keep her voice from traveling, "the talk is, that since you've done so well there as a manager, they're thinking of bringing you back to the home office and putting you in charge of a new department.

One to help bridge the gap between the home office and the store managers."

"I don't understand." Had Marcy heard right? Was she supposed to go back to the home office?

"It's something I've been pushing for years, you know that," Gail hurried on. "The company has gotten so big that the home office has lost touch with the customers. We don't know what they want anymore. The store managers know, but what good is that if they can't get their point across?"

"Oh, I agree," Marcy said, "but what's this new job?"

"You'll be in charge of—well, it's something like a glorified complaint department. Since you've had experience as a manager, you're just the person to handle this job. Of course, nothing's official, but I can guarantee you it's on the way. Then you'll be back here in Tampa. Won't that be wonderful?"

Marcy's head whirled with a myriad of dizzying sensations. It was an honor to be selected to head up a new department and, frankly, Marcy felt she deserved it. Still . . .

"Gosh Gail, I don't know what to say. This is such a shock. It's the last thing in the world I expected."

"Listen, if you think this is a shock, wait until you hear the salary increase that goes with it, but I won't tell you now. I'll know more about it tomorrow. Give me a ring then."

"Oh, yeah, sure," Marcy murmured, still a little numb.

"Who knows?" Gail exclaimed. "You might be back here by the end of the month. Won't that be terrific?"

"Terrific," she echoed with a sigh.

# Chapter Ten

Marcy was so excited with the idea of the promotion that she could hardly drive home. To think that the Super S was considering her for the job of coordinator between store managers and company administration! She could hardly wait to tell Drew. He'd be so proud of her, he'd sweep her into his arms and cover her with kisses and tell her he'd always known she could do it. It wouldn't be at all like telling Roger, who had never passed up an opportunity to belittle her achievements. She could almost hear him now.

"Well, it's very nice, Marcy—that is, if you plan on spending the rest of your life in a grocery store."

Well it wasn't Roger who was coming for dinner tonight. He was out of her life forever, and good riddance. And to think she'd almost let him destroy the most precious thing in her life, her love for Drew. As she buzzed around the kitchen preparing her gourmet dinner Marcy was filled with mixed emotions. As elated as she was over the job offer, she knew she'd never take it. Marcy was happy where she was and had never really been interested in moving into an upper management position. And now there was Drew as well.

If she took the job in Tampa, which was almost three hundred miles from Ft. Lauderdale, she'd have to move, and that meant she'd only see Drew on week-ends. He'd become such an integral part of her life that she couldn't imagine being away from him even for a few days. So despite the excitement and the honor of being offered a new job, she knew she'd never take it. Still, it was nice to know the Super S appreciated her.

Drew arrived early, as she'd expected, looking every inch like a Greek god with his lean torso and his tawny-gold hair tumbling across his forehead. She could feel the radiance of his masculinity, which tonight seemed to be charged with a special kind of buoyancy. Marcy could feel her heart jump in her chest, but she made no effort to suppress it. She enjoyed the strange inner excitement Drew brought to her.

"Mmm, it smells good in here," he said as soon as he stepped through the door.

"I hope so. We're having something special tonight."

Reaching out his long arms, he gathered her against his warm pulsing body. "Every night is special with you."

Wrapping her arms around him, Marcy locked herself into his embrace. "Do you know that you have a marvelous knack for always saying the right thing at the right time?"

"Mmm, yes, I know that," he murmured as his lips closed over hers. Marcy could feel her body surrendering to the burning sweetness of his kiss and responded freely, tightening her grip. Finally, reluctantly, she twisted her head to one side.

"I hate to be the wet blanket," she joked, "but even *we* have to eat once in a while." She stepped back a little and looked up at him, her eyes dancing with excitement. "I want you to know I've prepared a casserole extraordinaire to celebrate this auspicious occasion."

"I thought something was up."

"I even have a bottle of champagne on ice."

"What are we celebrating? Hurricane survival week?"

"No, but it is job-related."

He lifted a quizzical brow. "That's odd. I have a job-related surprise myself."

"Really?" Had he heard something already? she wondered.

"I had a visit from Joe Ashe this afternoon. He's one of the partners in our new office. It seems the space is available right now. He wanted to know if I wanted to start early."

Putting a hand on her hip, Marcy spun around. "Start early!" she exclaimed. "What does that mean?"

"It means instead of waiting until September, we start in August. What's wrong with that?"

Marcy opened her mouth as if to speak and then closed it again. Finally she said, "I can't believe you said that. What's wrong is that you're leaving me without an assistant."

"You can always train one. After all, you trained me."

"But I haven't been looking for anyone. You said you were going to leave in September. This is still June. What do you expect me to do for July and August?"

Drew's brow creased with annoyance. "For God's sake, Marcy, it's not as if I'm leaving without notice. You've known ever since the day I started I'd only be at the store for a few months."

"Are you going to stay until I can find someone?" Her voice held a note of disbelief.

Suddenly Drew turned and teasingly grazed his knuckle against her cheek. "All right, if that's what you want. But you don't have far to look, you know.

Mort could step into that job tomorrow and take over where I left off."

"I hadn't thought about him," she murmured, trying to hide the sinking feeling in the pit of her stomach. She didn't want Drew to leave so soon, but it was childish to hope he'd stay. He had his own career to pursue and she'd always known that.

"Mort's tailor-made for the job," he was saying. "Now how about opening that champagne?"

"It's right here."

"What about your surprise?" he asked as he started to work on the cork. "Or am I supposed to guess?"

"No. When I called the main office this afternoon, Gail told me that they're thinking of opening a new division to bridge the communication gap between the company officials and the store managers."

"Sounds reasonable." Drew nodded.

"I think it's a terrific idea. They should have done it years ago." Marcy's spirits began to rise a little. "Anyway, they want me to be in charge of it."

Drew put the bottle down in the sink and turned to her, his face an inscrutable mask. "In charge of it? What does that mean?"

"It means exactly what it implies." She was a little irritated at his lack of enthusiasm. "They want me to be in charge of the new division. Gail said that my experience as a store manager plus nine years in the main office made me a natural for the job."

Drew slapped his hand down on the counter. "And you're going to *take* it? You're going to move, just like that?" His face was flushed with anger.

"Wait a minute!" Marcy interrupted, her own temper rising out of control. "I never said I was going to take the job."

"Oh, but you will." He scowled. "Your advancement in management means everything to you. The Super

S comes first in your life, doesn't it? If someone in Tampa says they want you to move to the western side of the state, you're packed and ready."

Marcy's eyes blazed with anger as well as the sting of hurt and resentment. "What the hell do you mean by that?" she demanded. "It seems to me that you're pretty quick to prejudge. Someone offers me another job and immediately you jump to the conclusion that—"

"Jump to conclusions!" he repeated sarcastically. "No, I don't think so. Everyone knows about your total devotion to the Super S. I just happened to be the one and only person stupid enough to believe that other things were just as, if not more, important to you."

Marcy's expression darkened warningly. "Is there something wrong with company loyalty?" she demanded.

He leaned toward her, his expression sarcastic. "You know something, Marcy? I don't think you know the meaning of the word 'loyalty.' All you want to do is get out of here as fast as you can so that you can pursue your goals. And if that's loyalty, thank God I don't have it."

Fury flashed across her face. "You're right," she snapped, "you don't have it! It' s all right for you to walk off the job, but—"

"What do you mean, walk off the job? I said I'd stay until you got Mort trained!"

"Did it ever occur to you I might not *want* Mort?"

"Then did it ever occur to you to start training someone else?"

His tone infuriated her. It had a demeaning ring to it that set Marcy's teeth on edge. She glared at him. "I'm quite capable of figuring that out for myself."

Rancor sharpened her voice. "You seem to forget that I'm not an idiot who can't handle my job."

"I'd never question that," he snapped. "Anyone who is as career-oriented as you are is destined to reach the top. I guess I never realized until now exactly how determined you were." He shot her a disdainful look. "I'm glad this came up. It shows me a side of you I've never seen before."

"Perhaps we've both been mistaken," she lashed back, almost choking on her own words. The pain and anger in her was so great she hardly knew what she was saying.

Their eyes met and held. Drew's were as deep and stormy as the sea and hers were olive black and unfathomable. The silence hung between them like a heavy shroud.

Drew was the first to speak. His voice sounded like an empty void and dreadfully final. "I think you're right, Marcy. I think we've misjudged each other."

Without another word, he turned and walked out of the kitchen, through the apartment and out of her life. He closed the door behind him with a quiet finality.

Marcy slumped into the nearest chair, stunned at this sudden and devastating turn of events. She couldn't believe that just thirty minutes ago her mind had been brimming with glorious dreams for their future. And now? She dropped her hands into her lap. They lay there, as empty and vacuous as her heart. Swallowing a sob in her throat, her gaze fell on the candles on the table. They were still burning, still waiting expectantly for the love and laughter. As she watched them trembling in a slight breeze she reached back, back into her mind where she had sealed the door and turned to her own world that was as secure as a fortified tower. She sat there for a long while, and then, slowly, cautiously, she opened the door in her mind and looked inside.

She saw Roger lowering his newspaper to peer at her over the top of his glasses. "You realize, of course, that you'll have to stay here until I can find an apartment for us and line up a job for you," he'd said.

She had agreed, but it was during those three months of waiting that she realized how wonderful life was without him. When she'd brought up the subject of divorce, he agreed readily. Too readily, she realized now. Looking back with blunt honesty, she had to admit that she hadn't left Roger.

He had left her.

Somehow, Marcy had always known this, though she'd never dared admit it before. She'd buried it deep in her subconscious, not realizing it bubbled under there like a hidden spring waiting for that certain shift in the earth that would free it from its bondage. Well, the shift had come, all right. And the parallel was obvious—if one husband left her, wouldn't the next one do the same?

Leaning over, she blew out the candles. "Not necessarily," she said aloud, her voice stern and admonishing. She stood up. What was the matter with her anyway? She could handle a few bumps without crumbling to pieces. So she'd made a few mistakes, who hadn't? After all, she wasn't a superwoman. She was a human being subject to all the frailties of the species as well as their strengths. Whatever happened to those strengths, anyway, she wondered? Why, all of a sudden, was she sitting here moping when normally she'd be wrestling for a solution?

Marcy knew the answer rested within herself. This was no time to guard her precious pride at all costs. She'd let the man she loved, the man she wanted to spend the rest of her life with, walk out that door.

"You're a fool!"

Squaring her shoulders, Marcy put her chin up and her eyes glowed with determination. Suddenly, Marcy Jamison was in charge again. And it was about time!

Dashing into the bathroom, she started splashing water on her tearstained face. She threw on a little makeup and hastily pushed her hair around. She wasn't quite sure what she was going to say to Drew, but she was sure something would come to her before she reached his apartment. As she hurried, her fingers began to tremble with excitement as a little voice within said, "Be calm. Take it easy," and another voice answered, "But if you don't hurry, it may be too late."

She was reminded of the expression "hit the ground running" as she slammed the door behind her and bolted across the lot to her car. Revving the engine mercilessly, she shot out of the garage and squealed down the drive to the street. As she drove to Drew's apartment she planned her entrance. He'd be shocked to see her, but she knew he'd never refuse to talk to her. She'd be very calm and rational and he would listen. He was a wonderful listener.

Pulling up in front of his building, she parked the car and switched off the ignition. As she got out she looked up to the second floor. There were lights in Drew's apartment. He was home. A sudden pulsing lurch tugged at her heart. How could she have ever doubted him?

Hurrying now, she went around to his entrance at the back of the building. There were no lights anywhere and she had to guess her way. Stepping on twigs and leaves and brushing aside fallen branches, she finally reached the end of the building, but it was so dark, she couldn't even make out the staircase. Keeping her hands before her, she groped blindly, stumbling several times over debris from the storm, until at last her fingers made contact with something solid; the stair railing.

More confident now, Marcy paused to give her hair another hasty pat. Then taking a deep breath, she ran lightly up the steps until she tumbled into something thick and heavy and immovable. She tried to step around it. Her foot slipped; she felt herself falling.

"Drew! Drew!" she cried out as she tried to grab the first thing her hand touched. It was coarse and wet and unyielding. She felt herself falling into it.

Suddenly a light came on from above and Marcy heard footsteps thundering down the stairs. "Marcy, is that you?" came Drew's voice.

"Of course it's me," she grumbled. She was still trying to get a foothold and put her leg over—suddenly she heard the rending tear of her skirt. "Oh, damn!"

"It's you all right," came his voice from above.

Then his arms were around her waist and he was lifting her up and away from the wet mass beneath her.

"Slide back down," he directed, his grip tightening. "This way."

"I'll fall."

"Let go, will you?"

She felt herself toppling backward into Drew's arms. There was a lurch, a bump, and then they were crashing to the grass in a tangled heap. Marcy landed on top of Drew and started to squirm to an upright position, but his arm was in the way, and then his leg, and then his other arm as he pulled her toward him, strong and wondrously possessive.

"Drew!" she admonished, but there was no sting in her voice. There was only an awareness of his muscular body, the familiar scent of his after-shave, the pulsing knot in her stomach. He made no effort to get up or to let her up, but she managed to struggle to a sitting position.

"I've ripped my skirt and I'm sopping wet," she complained, trying to brush the clinging leaves and twigs from her blouse. "What the hell *is* that thing anyway?"

"My mattress."

"Mattress! Isn't it a little inconvenient out here?"

"The ceiling in my bedroom leaked and it got saturated. I was so damn mad, I threw it out the door."

"Temper, temper," she scolded with a laugh. Pushing a strand of wet hair off her face, Marcy looked down at him. He lay on his back, watching her with those keen, probing eyes she knew so well. She wondered if he had any idea how sensual he looked just now or how her blood was soaring. She made a feeble attempt to get up, but stopped when she felt his warm hand grip her knee. Drew raised himself up on one elbow.

"Are you all right?" he asked. His voice was like a caress.

She had to swallow the lump in her throat before she could trust her voice. "I'm fine," she murmured.

For a moment, there was a silence between them. Then Drew reached up and pulled her into his arms, cradling her head against his shoulder. He kissed her on the forehead.

"I guess I have some explaining to do," he whispered. "I didn't mean to fly off the handle like that."

She rested her head back against his arm. "I was just going to say the same thing."

"When you mentioned going to Tampa, it was like you were saying good-bye." She could feel his fingers twisting a lock of her hair. It was probably an unconscious gesture, but to Marcy it was more intimate than words. "I guess all along I've thought of this as a typical summer romance, a fleeting thing, easily forgotten." Pressing her hand against his chest, he stroked her hair. "I should have known better. We've shared too many precious moments for that. But still, I resisted loving you."

"I didn't know that," she murmured, "but I wondered why you'd never said you loved me. Well"—she shrugged—"I never said it either."

He started to sit up, pulling her with him. "You know something? I think we were both hung up on the same thing. Our ex-spouses."

She tried straightening her skirt, but somehow his leg was in the way. "Well, I don't know about you, but Roger sure fouled me up. I don't know why in hell I let him do that. I kept comparing him with you all the time, and you're nothing at all alike. He was such a nitpicker. . . ."

She was sitting between his legs with her back to him. Drew circled his arms around her body and locked them across her chest. "I know. He was hypercritical, and they're hard to live with." She could feel his breath in her hair, warm and exciting. "But think of me. I had just the opposite. Adele couldn't care less what I did or where I went. All she was interested in was her golf."

"Seems like a pretty shallow person."

"That's exactly what I thought, until recently, I read in the sports section that she'd joined the professional golf circuit."

Marcy tried to twist her head to look back at him. "What's wrong with that?"

"Nothing, except that I see now why she wanted to get rid of me. I was encumbering her career."

"Are you bitter about that, Drew?"

He nudged her playfully in the ribs. "Believe me, I'm not sorry about the way things turned out. I just feel duped, that's all. It's hard on the ego to have to admit that someone walked out on you."

Marcy leaned her head back against his shoulder and exhaled a long sigh. "Join the club. I didn't realize until tonight that Roger had done the same thing. Like Adele, he didn't come right out and say he wanted a divorce, but now that I think back, who am I kidding?"

"Do you think he took that job in Dallas just to get away from you?"

"I'm sure of it," she whispered.

Drew nudged her playfully in the ribs. "I'll have to remember that."

"Dog," she said as she started to get up, but Drew caught her hand and pulled her back down beside him. Then he rolled onto his back, lifting her with him. The grass was wet, but neither of them cared as they clung to each other, their blood racing crazily through their veins. As Drew's lips met hers Marcy could feel familiar currents of desire racing through her. As his mouth moved over hers, devouring its softness, she surrendered completely to his fiery possession.

Suddenly they were startled by the glare of lights in the apartment below Drew's.

Marcy lifted her head. "I think your landlord is getting worried."

"Landlady," he corrected, "and she's not worried, she's just nosy." He got up, pulling her with him. "Why don't we finish this upstairs?"

"You're so subtle."

"It's never been my strong point, but we still haven't discussed the core of our argument—your promotion and my partnership."

"I had no intentions of leaving," she assured him, "but I knew you misunderstood me when I told you about the promotion. Witch that I am, I deliberately let you go on thinking I was leaving you. Somehow my pride couldn't stand the thought of *you* leaving *me*."

"So you beat me to the punch."

"Something like that. I'm sorry."

He slapped at her skirt, brushing off leaves and grass. "Well, I can understand that, but I've been thinking it over. I realize that you have as much right to accept that promotion as I have to go into business for myself."

"Now you're really complicating things. Besides, the job hasn't been offered to me, just hinted at."

The light in the lower apartment went out as suddenly as it had gone on.

"Let's get out of here," Marcy whispered.

"Good idea." With three long steps, Drew reached the staircase, grabbed the mattress and threw it over the railing. It landed on the grass with a soggy squish.

"I'll say one thing"—Marcy laughed—"it beats any burglar alarm system I've ever seen."

"Maybe I can get a patent." Putting his arm around her, they started up the stairs, leaning into each other, completely oblivious to their wet, grass-stained clothes.

As they reached the porch Drew hugged her affectionately. "I've been sitting up here thinking about us since I got home, and I've come to the conclusion that it isn't fair to ask you to give up your career." With one swing of his arm, he pulled the two lounge chairs side by side and together they sank into the cushioned seats. "So," he went on, "I've decided not to go into partnership with my friends. Tomorrow morning, I'm driving over to Tampa to look around for an opening." His long, sensitive fingers trailed down her cheek and under her jawline. The sensuality of Drew's touch made her body tingle with awareness.

Suddenly he grinned and pulled her closer. "Here's one career woman I intend to keep."

Marcy's whole world reached out to encompass this man she loved so completely. As she reached up to smooth his hair back from his face her gaze misted over. Then her eyes moved into his, into the liquid blue shadows that were looking at her with an adoration that matched her own. Knowing he was willing to give up so much for her made Marcy realize how much he loved her.

She shook her head. "I'm not going to Tampa," she said. "I'm staying right here."

He gave her an affectionate slap on the thigh. "I don't think this martyr role suits either one of us. Why don't we just draw straws?"

"Because with my luck, I'll probably win, and I don't *want* to go back to Tampa. I never have, Drew. I'm perfectly happy here in Ft. Lauderdale managing the little Super S, doing my thing." Flicking a few leaves off his shirt, she massaged his shoulder in a gentle, circular pattern. "As much as I hate to admit it, Roger was right about one thing. I simply don't have the drive it takes to get to the top and stay there."

Even in the dim light, she could see the amusement dancing in his eyes. "Now that's a new line. I haven't heard it before."

"Well, it's true. I'm one of those people who lack aggression, but I'm not sorry that I do."

He slid a hand under the neckline of her dress. 'That's all right. I have enough for both of us."

"Tell me about it." She laughed, nudging him playfully in the ribs.

As his hand slid lower Marcy felt her breath catch in her throat. She retaliated by skimming her hand under his-shirt and rubbing the coarse hair on his chest. She reveled in the feel of his hard muscles under her exploring touch.

Laughing, Drew nuzzled a kiss against her throat. He was as ecstatic as she was, and as sexually aroused, too. "If we stay here in Ft. Lauderdale, do you think you can manage the Super S without me?"

"Very well."

"What would you say to the idea of not working at all? I'm one of those men who wants my wife home, waiting for me with open arms and wearing a thin pink negligee," he joked.

"Is that right?" she said dryly, leaning back to see him better. "And what about a bed to put her in?"

"You have a point. I forgot about that. But I have a nice, wide couch. Do you want to see it?"

"I believe you."

Suddenly Drew was on his feet, pulling her with him. "Come on, let's celebrate my retirement from the grocery world. I have some clean glasses on hand. Too bad you didn't think to bring the champagne."

"When I started out, I wasn't sure we'd be celebrating." Marcy felt so light-headed that she started to giggle. "I hope you realize that all employees retirement celebrations such as this must go into my weekly report to the home office."

Drew's hand moved intimately across her hip. "In that case, my love, why don't we show off a little to impress them?"

Marcy sighed with contentment. "I'd love it. So will Gail when she reads the report. . . ."

# RAPTURE ROMANCE

*Provocative and sensual,
passionate and tender—
the magic and mystery of love
in all its many guises*

## Coming next month

**WISH ON A STAR by Katherine Ransom.** Fighting for independence from her rich, domineering father, Vanessa Hamilton fled to Maine—and into the arms of Rory McGee. Drawn to his strong masculinity, his sensuous kisses ignited her soul. But she had only just tasted her new-found freedom—was she willing to give herself to another forceful man?

**FLIGHT OF FANCY by Maggie Osborne.** A plane crash brought Samantha Adams and Luke Bannister together for a short, passionate time. But they were rivals in the air freight business, and even though Luke said he loved her and wanted to marry her, Samantha was unsure. Did Luke really want her—or was he only after Adams Air Freight?

**ENCHANTED ENCORE by Rosalynn Carroll.** Vicki Owens couldn't resist Patrick Wallingford's fiery embrace years ago, and now he was back reawakening a tantalizing ecstasy. Could she believe love was forever the second time around, or was he only using her to make another woman jealous?

**A PUBLIC AFFAIR by Eleanor Frost.** Barbara Danbury told herself not to trust rising political star Morgan Newman. But she was lost when he pledged his love to her in a night of passion. Then scandal shattered Morgan's ideal image and suddenly Barbara doubted everything—except her burning hunger for him. . . .

**TELL US YOUR OPINIONS AND RECEIVE A FREE COPY OF THE RAPTURE NEWSLETTER.**

Thank you for filling out our questionnaire. Your response to the following questions will help us to bring you more and better books. In appreciation of your help we will send you a free copy of the Rapture Newsletter.

1. Book Title:_____

   Book #:_____ (5-7)

2. Using the scale below how would you rate this book on the following features? Please write in one rating from 0–10 for each feature in the spaces provided. Ignore bracketed numbers.

   (Poor) 0 1 2 3 4 5 6 7 8 9 10 (Excellent)
   
                              0–10 Rating

   Overall Opinion of Book. . . . . . . . . . . . . . . . . _____ (8)
   Plot/Story. . . . . . . . . . . . . . . . . . . . . . . . . . _____ (9)
   Setting/Location. . . . . . . . . . . . . . . . . . . . . _____ (10)
   Writing Style. . . . . . . . . . . . . . . . . . . . . . . . _____ (11)
   Dialogue. . . . . . . . . . . . . . . . . . . . . . . . . . . _____ (12)
   Love Scenes. . . . . . . . . . . . . . . . . . . . . . . . _____ (13)
   Character Development:
   Heroine:. . . . . . . . . . . . . . . . . . . . . . . . . . . _____ (14)
   Hero:. . . . . . . . . . . . . . . . . . . . . . . . . . . . . _____ (15)
   Romantic Scene on Front Cover. . . . . . . . . _____ (16)
   Back Cover Story Outline . . . . . . . . . . . . . . _____ (17)
   First Page Excerpts. . . . . . . . . . . . . . . . . . . _____ (18)

3. What is your: Education:   Age:_____(20-22)

       High School  (  )1    4 Yrs. College (  )3
       2 Yrs. College (  )2    Post Grad    (  )4 (23)

4. Print Name:_____

   Address:_____

   City:_____State:_____Zip:_____

   Phone # (    ) _____ (25)

   Thank you for your time and effort. Please send to New American Library, Rapture Romance Research Department, 1633 Broadway, New York, NY 10019.

# YOUR CHOICE OF TWO RAPTURE ROMANCE BOOK CLUB PACKAGES.

(A) Four Rapture Romances plus two Signet Regency Romances

*or*

(B) Four Rapture Romances, one Signet Regency Romance and one Scarlet Ribbons Romance

Whichever package you choose save $.60 off the combined cover prices plus get a free Rapture Romance, for a total savings of $2.55.

**To start you off, we'll send you four books absolutely FREE** The total value of all four books is $7.80, but they're yours *free* even if you never buy another book.

So order Rapture Romances today. And prepare to meet a different breed of man.

## YOUR FIRST 4 BOOKS ARE FREE!

### Just Mail The Coupon Below

------------------------------------------------

**Rapture Romance, P.O. Box 996, Greens Farms, CT 06436**

Please send me the 4 Rapture Romances described in this ad FREE and without obligation. Unless you hear from me after I receive them, send me 6 NEW Romances to preview each month. I understand that you will bill me for only 5 of them with no shipping, handling or other charges. I always get one book FREE every month. There is no minimum number of books I must buy, and I can cancel at any time. The first 4 FREE books are mine to keep even if I never buy another book.

Each month please send me package ( )A      ( )B

| | |
|---|---|
| Name | (please print) |

| | |
|---|---|
| Address | City |

| | | |
|---|---|---|
| State | Zip | Signature (if under 18, parent or guardian must sign) |

 *RAPTURE ROMANCE*

This offer, limited to one per household and not valid to present subscribers, expires June 30, 1984. Prices subject to change. Specific titles subject to availability. Allow a minimum of 4 weeks for delivery.

# RAPTURE ROMANCE

**Provocative and sensual,
passionate and tender—
the magic and mystery of love
in all its many guises**

*New Titles Available Now*

# RAPTURE ROMANCE

### Provocative and sensual, passionate and tender— the magic and mystery of love in all its many guises

# RAPTURE ROMANCE

*Provocative and sensual,
passionate and tender—
the magic and mystery of love
in all its many guises*

**Buy them at your local
bookstore or use coupon
on next page for ordering.**

# RAPTURE ROMANCE

### Provocative and sensual, passionate and tender— the magic and mystery of love in all its many guises

# RAPTURE ROMANCE

## Provocative and sensual, passionate and tender— the magic and mystery of love in all its many guises

---

**Buy them at your local**

**bookstore or use coupon**

**on next page for ordering.**